PEA'S BOOK
of
BIG
DREAMS

www.randomhousechildrens.co.uk

Also by Susie Day

Pea's Book of Best Friends

Coming soon

Pea's Book of Birthdays

PEA'S BOOK

of

BIG

DREAMS

  SUSIE DAY

RED FOX

Pea's Book of Big Dreams
A RED FOX BOOK 978 1 782 95174 2

First published in Great Britain by Red Fox Books,
an imprint of Random House Children's Publishers UK
A Random House Group Company

This edition published 2013

1 3 5 7 9 10 8 6 4 2

The Random House Group Limited supports The Forest Stewardship Council® (FSC®), the
leading international forest-certification organisation. Our books carrying the FSC label are
printed on FSC®-certified paper. FSC is the only forest-certification scheme supported by the
leading environmental organisations, including Greenpeace. Our paper procurement policy
can be found at www.randomhouse.co.uk/environment

Set in 13/18pt Baskerville MT by Falcon Oast Graphic Art

Red Fox Books are published by Random House Children's Publishers UK,
61–63 Uxbridge Road, London W5 5SA

www.**randomhousechildrens**.co.uk
www.**totallyrandombooks**.co.uk
www.**randomhouse**.co.uk

Addresses for companies within The Random House Group Limited can be found at:
www.randomhouse.co.uk/offices.htm

THE RANDOM HOUSE GROUP Limited Reg. No. 954009

A CIP catalogue record for this book is available from the British Library.

Printed and bound in Great Britain by
CPI Group (UK) Ltd, Croydon CR0 4YY

For my mum and dad,
who let me have big dreams

CHAPTER 1

THE NEW VITÓRIA

'Ow!' said Tinkerbell.

'I'm making you look well-behaved – like you go to bed on time without whining— *Shush*,' said Clover, fastening the top button of Tinkerbell's only-for-best shirt.

'*Woof-woof-woof*,' said Wuffly, running in circles with a welly in her mouth.

'Can someone make the dog look like she's well-behaved and goes to bed on time too?' shouted Mum from upstairs.

Clover and Tinkerbell both looked at Pea.

With a sigh, Pea retrieved the welly and shut

Wuffly in the kitchen. Then she sat on the bottom stair, clutching a sheaf of typed pages, and waited nervously for the doorbell to ring. This was going to be a big day.

Last year, the Llewellyn family had lived in a little flat by the sea in Tenby, south-west Wales. But ever since they'd moved into the house with the raspberry-red front door in London, they had shared it with an au pair named Vitória. Vitória had done all the boring parental things, like making tea and shouting at Tinkerbell, whenever Mum was too busy being Marina Cove – famous author of the bestselling *Mermaid Girls* books – to be Mum as well. Pea used to talk to Vitória about all her troubles. Sometimes it was hard, being the sister in the middle. But with Vitória to talk to, Pea never felt the least bit overlooked.

Then, just before Christmas, Vitória had taken her caramel hair and her tiny coffee cups and her fluffy yellow dressing gown back to Brazil to live with her own family.

It was bad enough having that flat feeling that the end of December always brought. The house felt empty: no tall lit-up Christmas tree in the corner, no tinsel, no cards on strings or presents waiting to be unwrapped; only the occasional '*Ouch!*' as you stepped on an old pine needle.

But now they needed to find a new Vitória too.

A whole new person to live in the little flatlet off the kitchen and look after them.

A stranger, moving into their home.

Pea found it a very scary prospect.

At least Mum had agreed that – since it was *them* the new au pair would be looking after – the three sisters should help her choose a good one.

WANTED

Lovely live-in person to look after a family in Kensal Rise

We are: a mum, three girls and a dog.

You are: kind to sleepy people in the mornings.

You must love dogs even when they are too bouncy, and be able to make nice sandwiches. Ability to create twirly hairdos also an advantage.
Please don't apply if you are fussy or don't like mermaids.
To start: as soon as possible!

They had put an advert in the local paper, and five people who wanted to be new Vitórias had sent back a CV. (Apparently this meant *curriculum vitae*, which was posh Latin for a list of all the things a person had ever done that might be useful when it came to looking after a mum, three girls and a dog.) Pea had spent hours poring over them, in case there were any stern governesses like in books, with buns and tightly buttoned-up jackets and a ruler to check they were standing up straight. Vitória had never done anything like that, but she had been their first ever au pair, and Clover said that with new people you shouldn't be too trusting.

But the pile of CVs on Pea's lap was full of

identical promises to go on trips and enjoy cleaning the toilet. None of the replies said that they would lock naughty children in the cupboard under the stairs with the cobwebs, or wash anyone's mouth out with soap.

'I don't get why *we* have to get all dressed up,' said Tinkerbell, wriggling away from Clover, who was jabbing at her head with ugly flowery hairclips. 'Doesn't the new Vitória have to impress *us*?'

'Well, ye-es,' said Mum, appearing at the top of the stairs in her best shimmery silver skirt – the one that looked like a mermaid tail. 'But we have to impress them back too, my starlings. If they're extra-lovely, they'll be able to pick any family they like to live with. And they might not want one that smells of dog and yesterday's socks.'

'We do not smell of yesterday's socks!' said Clover hotly.

'Or dog!' protested Tinkerbell.

Clover sniffed the air in the hallway, then wrinkled her nose. 'Actually, we might smell a little bit dog-adjacent. I'll make some toast – that'll cover it up,' she said, hurrying to the kitchen.

'Won't they wonder why we're eating toast at eleven in the morning?' said Tinkerbell, watching Wuffly escape gleefully through the now-open kitchen door.

Mum looked panicked. 'They might think we've only just got up. They won't want to live with lazy children who don't get up. Clover, abort the toast! Abort the toast!'

Pea sighed. That was why they really needed a new Vitória: so someone else could be the sensible, organized one in the family instead of it always having to be her. She stood up and waved the top sheets from her pile of papers.

'Listen! I thought of that already,' she said. 'They all had to write CVs so we'd know if they were right for the job, so I wrote ours as well. Then they can tell if we've got the right qualifications for them too.'

Pea fanned out the pages for the others to see. Clover's was on top, since she was the eldest.

CLOVER
Age: 13
Current occupation: schoolgirl
Likes: musicals, expensive things she can't have, attention
Special skills: singing, piano
Future career: actor/director of plays

PEA
Age: 11
Current occupation: schoolgirl
Likes: books
Special skills: writing, reading, making sandwiches
Future career: writer (like Mum)

TINKERBELL
Age: 7
Current occupation: menace
Likes: Wuffly, mess, spiders
Special skills: escapology
Future career: ~~criminal mastermind~~
yet to be determined

Each CV was illustrated with a sketch by Pea's best friend, Sam One, the boy next door. They were excellent likenesses. Sam One had exactly captured Clover's pretty pink face and tumbling blonde hair, the image of her mother. Pea's picture was paper-pale and freckled, with red hair (though Sam One had been kind enough to smooth down her frizz, and her chin looked normal-sized instead of big and pointy). Tinkerbell was brown-skinned and fierce-looking, with black curls braided close to her head in a spiral.

'I was worried "criminal mastermind" might

8

put people off, so I crossed it out,' Pea explained, with a nervous glance at Tinkerbell. 'Anyway, seven is a bit young to be making career plans.'

'I think they're fabulous, Pea-pod. But where's mine?' said Mum, leaning down to rest her chin on Pea's shoulder.

'You don't need one. Everyone knows who you are,' said Pea, as Tinkerbell chased Wuffly back into the kitchen.

That wasn't *quite* true. Marina Cove wasn't the Hollywood-filmstar sort of famous. She didn't get followed around by photographers (much to Clover's dismay), or asked for her autograph (except for that one time in Tesco). But she got letters from adoring fans from all over the world. If you liked books, especially the mermaid sort, you'd definitely know Marina Cove.

Mum smiled regardless, and wrapped Pea in one of those fond, tight, jasmine-perfumed hugs that only she could give.

Then the doorbell rang.

'Places, everyone, places!' said Clover, clapping her hands.

They all stood in a line.

Clover fluffed up her hair and smiled sweetly.

Tinkerbell sulked.

Pea's insides felt slithery. She wanted Vitória to suddenly appear on the doorstep and say she wanted to live with them again after all. That was what would happen in a book, if she was writing it.

Pea shut her eyes and hoped.

But when Mum opened the front door, standing there was a willowy young woman with a scraped-back ponytail and a sweaty forehead, wearing a blue tracksuit.

'Oh,' said Clover, eyeing the woman's muddy trainers.

'*Hmmph*,' said Tinkerbell, undoing her too-tight collar and giving Clover a mean stare.

'Sorry,' panted the woman. 'I was out running, and then I have training, so no time to change.

Hello! I am Anna, from Poland – pleased to meet you.'

Anna shook hands with each of them, then followed Mum on a quick tour of the house. Then they all sat in the yellow-painted front room. Pea gave Anna their CVs, and waited anxiously while she read them. It had been hard to know what to include and what to miss out. Now that she was here, Pea realized Anna was bound to ask about their unusual names, and why they all looked so very different even though they were sisters, and Pea would have to go through the same old explanations about their dads, and why she was named after a small green vegetable.

(Clover's father had been Mum's childhood sweetheart, but he had died when Clover was a baby. All Pea knew about *her* father was that his name was Ewan McGregor – no, not that one – and that he'd run away the night she was born, leaving Mum all alone with two little ones on an island in Greece. Fortunately, Tinkerbell's dad, Clem, was plenty of dad for all three of them, even if he didn't live with them any more. As for the small green vegetable, Pea was technically a Prudence, but she used to have a lisp, and introducing yourself as 'Pwudenthe' is no fun at all.)

But instead, Anna asked, 'Who wrote these?' with a big smile.

Pea put up one hand, then blushed and put it down again when she remembered they weren't at school.

'Very clever thought, I like it,' said Anna.

'Thank you,' said Pea, glowing. Perhaps a new Vitória could be as nice as the old one, after all.

'Pea's ever so brainy,' said Clover. 'You won't have to help her with homework or anything like that.'

'Good!' said Anna. 'I have five brothers and sisters, all small, and I had to do theirs a lot. So I am quite fed up of homework, really.' She caught Mum's eye, then put her hand to her mouth with a gasp. 'I shouldn't say these things, though! I will help if you need help, of course.'

Mum laughed, and said that being fed up of homework was quite a normal way to be.

'Do you like singing?' said Clover. 'Or mind when it's someone practising who might not get all the notes exactly right yet?' (Clover had got *100 Songs from Stage and Screen* on CD for Christmas, and was learning them all, loudly.)

'I don't mind singing,' said Anna. 'If you wouldn't mind me joining in sometimes?'

Clover beamed. Vitória had been very good at twirly hairdos and rainbow nail polish, but she didn't sing.

'And you,' said Anna, turning to Tinkerbell. 'I bet you are not usually the quiet one, am I right? Is there anything you would like to ask me?'

Clover and Pea stiffened. Mum pressed her lips together in a tight pink line. Tinkerbell had taken a long time to get used to living in London, and had invented multiple ingenious schemes to force the family to move back to their old home in Tenby. Pea was fairly sure she was over all that now, but she'd put on her innocent face, and that was always worrying.

'If we play Monopoly,' said Tinkerbell, very seriously, 'will you let me win?'

Anna narrowed her eyes and gave Tinkerbell a serious look of her own. 'No,' she said.

Pea held her breath.

But Tinkerbell sat back with a grin. 'Good. I like her, Mum. Can she stay?'

Mum laughed, and looked apologetically at Anna. 'Oh, my horrible children and their total lack of manners. I'm sorry, Anna. We do actually have four other people to see . . .'

'If we hide behind the sofa when they ring the bell, they'll never know we're here,' said Clover.

'It's mean to waste their time, if we already know we want Anna, not them,' added Pea.

'I promise not to put any snakes in her bed,' said Tinkerbell. 'Real *or* plastic.'

Mum coughed, and gave Anna another rueful smile. 'That is actually quite a compliment. Which

I probably shouldn't have told you. Um ... I know this isn't how these things are supposed to be done, probably, but it looks like we want you: do *you* want *us*?'

Pea could already picture Anna taking Wuffly out for frosty runs across Queen's Park, then buying them pastries in the cosy little café. She would cook them Polish breakfasts (whatever they might be), and smile a lot, and stay for ever.

'Yes!' said Anna. 'Only – there are some times I am not free, because of running and training. I do a lot of running and training. For competitions. This would be OK, right?'

Clover, Pea and Tinkerbell all looked at Mum.

'Probably,' said Mum. 'What sort of times?'

'Well, I can't do mornings,' said Anna. 'Because I get up at six to go running. And then sometimes afternoons. And not Thursday evenings, or Tuesdays, or any time at all on Fridays. And once a month I have to go away for a few days. Or maybe a week. For training. In Poland.'

'Oh,' said Mum.

Being a writer, Mum mostly worked from home. But she often went to schools to talk about the *Mermaid Girls* books, or gave creative writing classes to adults – and even when she was at home, she needed to be able to shut her study door and think fishy thoughts. The new Vitória needed to be around in the mornings to take Tinkerbell to school, and afternoons to collect her again, and all sorts of other peculiar times.

There was nothing more to be said. It didn't matter how lovely she was: Anna couldn't possibly be the new Vitória.

Once Mum had explained, Anna shook hands solemnly with each of them, and they all said how sorry they were, and then she left, without Pea ever finding out what a Polish breakfast was. It was like saying goodbye to Vitória all over again, nearly. Tinkerbell sighed hard as the raspberry-red front door closed behind Anna. Clover gave a dramatic sniff. Pea clutched her thumbs tightly, to hold in all her disappointment.

'Chins up, chicklets,' said Mum, not sounding very bright herself. 'If our first interview went that well, we're bound to find someone just as perfect!'

But it was not to be.

New Vitória number two nodded a lot, but spoke no English.

New Vitória number three breezed in on platform heels, wearing a fabulous orange coat and the sort of eye make-up that people called 'striking', charming Clover at once. But the neat satchel that dangled from her elbow turned out to contain a tiny dog, which yipped wildly at Wuffly – who barked back – which meant more yipping – and then there was biting, and a very quick exit before Mum had asked any questions.

New Vitória number four didn't even turn up.

'Sorry, my sweeties,' said Mum. 'We're going to *have* to like this one.'

New Vitória number five marched into the

17

hall, announcing, 'You may call me Mrs Peach, children.'

She really did have a bun, and a tightly buttoned suit jacket, and Pea was certain she was eyeing the area under the stairs to see if there might be a suitable cupboard for keeping cobwebs and naughty children in. She sent Wuffly scurrying into the kitchen with a single steely glare. She declared that children had no place in making important family decisions, and shut the front-room door on them firmly. For an awful five minutes, with their left ears pressed against the closed door to listen, it seemed as if their fates were sealed. But then they overheard Mrs Peach telling Mum off for putting her tea mug on the table without using a coaster, and all was saved. (The Llewellyns had never been a coaster sort of family.)

Mum shook Mrs Peach's hand politely, but without smiling.

'We'll call you,' she said, waiting until Mrs Peach was well out of sight round the corner before slamming the front door closed.

'You won't, will you?' asked Pea.

'No!' said Mum. 'I'm not living with someone I have to call Mrs Peach! But what are we going to do? You all go back to school soon. I'm going to Manchester on Wednesday to talk to librarians, and I'll be late back, and then my creative-writing classes are all evenings this term. *And* I promised the Dreaditor I'd begin book five right away, only my head's still full of book four, and—'

'Where's Wuffly?' asked Tinkerbell, emerging from the kitchen.

'Oh no, she hasn't got over the back fence again, has she?' groaned Mum. 'Honestly, that dog . . .'

Outside, on the street, there was a yell, then a screech of car brakes and an awful smashing sound.

They all ran out.

'Oh no, oh no,' whispered Pea, clutching Tinkerbell's sleeve.

She could see a car stopped at a funny angle,

with little shattered bits of glass all across the bonnet.

There was a bicycle on its side with one wheel spinning, with a person sprawled beside it.

And there was Wuffly, lying between the two, very still.

CHAPTER

2

ACCIDENTS

'Wuffly!' howled Tinkerbell, running down the crazy paving.

Clover sprinted after her, yanking her back before she could run into the road. 'Careful – there could be more cars coming!'

Mum's face was white and shocked, but she swallowed hard, took Pea's hands, and squeezed them. 'I'll call 999, you go and fetch blankets and towels – as many as you can carry.'

But Pea couldn't move. It was as if her feet were stuck to the ground. She could see Tinkerbell kneeling on the tarmac, and hear Clover saying,

'Hello? Hello? Don't move, don't move,' and Mum running into the house, then coming back outside saying, 'Ambulance, please, and police, I think; there's been an accident,' and it was all happening so fast, but slow at the same time, like a dream. As if it wasn't real at all.

'Quick as you can, Pea!'

Pea shook herself, and ran back into the house and up the stairs as fast as she could. She pulled all the towels out of the airing cupboard. She grabbed Wuffly's best smelly blue blanket from Tinkerbell's bedroom floor. She took a very deep breath, then ran back outside into the freezing cold.

Tinkerbell was still kneeling over Wuffly, who lay terribly still. The bicycle's rider was trying to sit up, muttering something to Clover in a half-familiar foreign language, the cold air making her breath come out in little puffs of white. Mum was talking to the driver of the car, a bald man who was saying, 'I just didn't see – there was ice – I just didn't see . . .' over and over.

Part of Pea wanted to shut her eyes or run away – but she could hear Tinkerbell crying. It was time to be brave and grown up.

She ran to Tinkerbell's side, almost too terrified to look, but when she knelt down, she could see Wuffly's chest going up and down. Wuffly was making little whining sounds, and quivering, and one of her back legs was bent in a direction Pea was sure it wasn't meant to go, but her eyes were bright.

'Will she be OK?' whispered Tinkerbell.

'Of course she will,' said Pea in a confident voice, wrapping the blue blanket around Wuffly. It was strange: she didn't know really, not for sure – but somehow saying so made her believe it.

Tinkerbell obviously felt the same. She smiled at once, and put her nose next to Wuffly's. 'Silly dog, running into the road,' she said, and gently tugged one hairy grey ear.

Pea draped a warm towel over Tinkerbell's back, then carried the rest over to Clover.

'You're supposed to lie on your side, and not move in case you've broken your neck,' Clover was saying, a bit more crossly than Pea thought you were really meant to when someone had just been in a horrible accident.

'Honest, I'm fine,' the cyclist was saying now in a Londonish accent, tugging her cycle helmet off.

It was a woman, grown-up but young, with short pixie-like hair that had been dyed purple in patches, so that her head looked somehow leopard-printed. She had lots of earrings, a fuzzy turquoise coat, and the sort of cheerful grin that said getting knocked off a bicycle was the sort of thing that happened sometimes – but one of her ankles was twisted in an odd direction, just like Wuffly's. She didn't seem to feel it, though; when Pea tried draping a warm towel over her, she looked baffled.

'What's that for? I don't need—' She tried to sit up properly, but the moment she moved her left leg, her face turned quite green and her head fell back onto the icy tarmac, hard.

'See?' said Clover. 'I told you you were supposed to lie down!'

'Clover!' said Mum, who was now directing traffic.

But the bicycle woman was laughing – even if the laughing was broken up with ouches and groans. She rested her head on the pillow of towels Pea had made to keep her head off the cold ground. Pea was careful not to joggle her ankle.

'Don't worry, there's an ambulance coming,' she said. 'It'll be all right. It doesn't look too bad.'

Just like before, even though she didn't know anything about ankles, saying so in a confident voice seemed to make it true. Pea thought about going back inside to find the first-aid kit, but it was mostly plasters and safety pins, and a packet of sugar in case someone went diabetic. (They'd done it at school.)

'Are you diabetic?' Pea asked.

'No,' said the bicycle woman.

'What's your name?' asked Clover.

'Cloudier,' said the bicycle woman, confusingly. But Pea knew how annoying it was to always be asked about it when you had an unusual name, so she didn't say anything.

'Hey, little one,' Cloudier called over to Tinker-bell, her voice faint and croaky. 'Is your dog all right?'

Tinkerbell nodded, and Wuffly gave a little hopeful yelp, as if she agreed. Pea could see her head resting on Tinkerbell's knee, and felt a rush of relief.

'I'm so sorry – I don't know how she could have got out onto the road like that,' Mum began to say, but Cloudier shook her head as sirens began to wail in the distance.

'No big,' she said, grinning. 'Was, like, totally my fault. I overloaded my bike. And it's crazy icy out here. Car swerves to go round the dog, I try to swerve round the car – *boom*. Game over.'

Pea looked at the bicycle, still on its side in the middle of the road. It was the old-fashioned sort with a basket on the front. There were two fat panniers strapped to the rear wheel, a cardboard box taped to the back of the seat, and a big black canvas bag that seemed to have come off in the accident and was now lying under a parked car on the other side of the road.

'Oh . . . my bag,' said Cloudier, craning her neck, then groaning again as the sirens got louder.

'Is there something important inside?' asked Pea.

An odd intense look passed over Cloudier's face. 'Very important,' she said.

The ambulance – with full flashing blue lights, but now no siren – finally arrived. Two paramedics in green hopped out, a man and a woman. The man went over to the car, to check on the bald driver. The woman knelt down next to Cloudier, shining a little torch into her eyes and her ears, and asking her lots of questions.

'Can you help my dog?' called Tinkerbell, stroking the blue-wrapped bundle in her lap.

The paramedic man explained that they were for humans only, and that they'd have to call a vet – which was unfortunate. No one ever said 'vet' in front of Wuffly. It was always 'the vee-ee-tee' or 'the Special V Lady', or Wuffly would howl and growl and suddenly demonstrate remarkable acceleration and hiding-under-the-bed powers. Today, she tried the same, only with a poorly leg. The blue-wrapped bundle ended up a whimpering heap in Tinkerbell's arms.

'Take her inside, darlings, before she hurts herself more,' said Mum. 'We'll get a taxi to you-know-where as soon as we can.'

As Clover was helping Tinkerbell to carry Wuffly up the drive, the police arrived.

Then everything seemed to happen at once.

Cloudier was put on a stretcher and carried into the back of the ambulance.

Mum talked to the police officer about how it

was icy, and probably wasn't all Wuffly's fault really, and the police officer wrote some of it down.

A big truck came to tow away the car with the smashed windscreen.

Then the ambulance left, and the police officer drove off with the car's driver, and suddenly it was just them, lots of towels, and a bicycle piled with stuff.

'Shouldn't the police have taken that stuff away with them too?' asked Pea.

'Probably,' said Mum. 'It's not like Cloudier could have put it all in the ambulance with her. We'll have to take in her bags, anyway: we can't leave all her things out in the road. They might be valuable.'

While Mum and Clover carefully wheeled the bicycle onto their crazy-paving driveway, Pea fetched the black canvas bag that was still lying under the car. *Very important*, Cloudier had said. What could possibly be in there? There was a square white label in a tag hanging from the bag's strap.

KLAUDIA WENDT

CAC

020 823 909

'Oh,' said Pea to herself. 'Not Cloudier. *Klaudia*.'

That evening they had a Chinese takeaway – Pea's favourite – as a calming-down treat.

The Paget-Skidelskys came over to help them eat it. They were the family who lived next door: Dr Genevieve Paget and Dr Kara Skidelsky, Family Therapists and Child Psychologists (as it said on the gold plaque at the end of their drive-way), and their twins Sam One and Sam Two. Sam One was a boy and Sam Two was a girl – but they had identical floppy dark hair, and today they were wearing matching hand-knitted jumpers in orange and green.

'It sounds terrible,' said Dr Paget, scooping rice onto each plate as Clover told them the story in full gory detail. 'Will poor Wuffly be all right?'

Tinkerbell nodded wanly as Mum explained that she was spending the night at the vee-ee-tee after having an operation on her leg.

'And Tink was very brave, holding her paw while they gave her the anaesthetic, weren't you, Stinks?'

No one else seemed to notice, but Pea thought she saw Sam Two roll her eyes, which was strange. Sam Two wasn't always especially nice, but she'd always liked Tinkerbell. They both enjoyed discovering what melted in the microwave, or putting beetles into matchboxes to scare people with.

After they'd shared out rice, and chicken in sticky yellow bean sauce, Mum passed around a plate of crunchy spring rolls. After everybody had taken one, there was still one left over.

Sam Two's hand snaked out to grab it, but was swatted away by Dr Paget.

'I need extra energy!' said Sam Two. 'I'm in training!'

'Sam's joined the Kensal Rise Kites,' explained Dr Skidelsky. 'The girls' football team I train.'

31

'Ooh,' said Tinkerbell, her eyes going wide. 'Can *I* join?'

'No,' said Sam Two sharply. 'It's not for *babies*.'

Everyone noticed that time. After a lot of whispering from that end of the table, Sam Two muttered a reluctant 'Sorry.'

'I think Pea should have the last spring roll,' said Mum, dropping it onto Pea's plate. 'After today, I think she's earned it.'

'You *were* amazing, Pea,' said Clover. 'I've always thought I'd be the good one in a crisis. I thought it would be like directing a play, telling people where to go and what to do. But I was sure I was going to be sick when I saw Klaudia's leg, sticking out all crooked. And Wuffly's. And *you* weren't bothered one bit.' She was staring at Pea intently, almost suspiciously, as if she might not be Pea at all.

'I *was* bothered,' Pea said guiltily. She'd had to tell herself to be brave. 'All I did was bring down some towels.'

'Rubbish!' said Mum. 'Clover's right. You stayed

32

calm. You said all the right things. We'd have been hopeless without you.'

'Perhaps you've got a budding doctor in the family, eh?' said Dr Paget, giving Pea a warm smile.

Pea smiled back weakly. It felt lovely, having all these nice things being said about her – but she wouldn't want to have to be that brave every day.

'Don't be silly, Mum Gen,' said Sam One. 'Pea's going to be a writer. It says so on her CV.'

They all turned to look at the fridge, where the three CVs were now pinned up with magnets.

'So it does,' said Dr Paget. 'Well, you'll definitely have something to write about now!'

Pea looked at the printed words on the fridge door and felt relieved at once. She took a very large bite of spring roll, and by the time she'd finished chewing they were talking about Mrs Peach again, and blaming the accident on her. After they'd finished, everyone else went to drink coffee in the front room, but Pea and Sam One stayed in the kitchen to work on their story together.

Pea opened the new rainbow notebook she'd bought with her Christmas money. She was in the middle of writing a series of stories about a girl called Sky, who ate nothing but mashed potato and lived on the moon. Sam One was doing the pictures. Clover and Tinkerbell had read the first one – *A Girl Called Sky* was the title – and reviewed it as 'quite clever' and 'almost as good as Mum's', so she'd entered it into *Spark!* magazine's young writers' competition, online. She was already working on three sequels while waiting to see if she'd won.

'Was it really horrible, seeing a broken ankle?' asked Sam One as he sketched out a moonscape.

'Quite horrible,' said Pea. 'But your Mum Gen's right. Writers probably need to have lots of experiences – otherwise they'd have to think of all their ideas just out of their imaginations.'

As if to prove it, she turned over a new page in her notebook and began to write.

The Unexpected Arrival
by Pea Llewellyn

Sky was woken up in the middle of the night by a
terrible crunching noise.

'What can that be, Moon-dog?' she said, and
dashed outside.

In the starlight, she could see a crashed
spaceship. It had landed in her tree.

'Ow! Help! Ow!' shouted a nice-seeming lady
with puffy purple hair like a cloud.

Sky was frightened, but she did a large number
of very heroic things like climbing up the tree and
fixing the spaceship so it could fly to the ground.
Even Moon-dog looked impressed.

'What's your name?' asked Sky.

'Cloudier,' said the lady. 'Ow!' she said again.

'Come inside and have some mashed potato,'
said Sky. 'That makes everything feel better.'

The next morning, the vee-ee-tee rang to say

35

that Wuffly had woken up and was ready to come home.

Mum and Tinkerbell went off to fetch her, and came back by taxi. She looked most forlorn, with one back leg in plaster, and a cone around her neck to stop any chewing – but she was home safe.

'Do you think Klaudia will be able to go home from the hospital today too?' asked Pea.

'Maybe;' said Clover. 'Either way, she's going to need her things back.'

Klaudia's bicycle was in the back garden, and all her bags and boxes were piled up in the hallway – including the mysterious black canvas bag with the *very important* something inside.

While Mum and Tinkerbell got Wuffly settled in the front room on her old blue blanket, Clover called the number written on the label.

'Klaudia? She doesn't live here any more!' shouted a man's voice, loud enough for Pea to hear it from across the room. 'Don't call here again!'

'Well, that was rude. Never mind, we'll call the

hospital,' said Clover confidently. 'Then we can leave her a message.'

But none of the nearby hospitals would tell her if they had a patient called Klaudia Wendt.

They both stared at the black canvas bag.

'It wouldn't be *too* nosy to look inside,' said Clover. 'Just so we can make sure she gets it back.'

They lifted it onto the hall table. It was surprisingly heavy.

Pea undid one buckle. Clover undid the other.

They lifted the flap.

There was something silver inside, and round. No, not round exactly; it was a cylinder – a fat one, with a silver top and a handle and some kind of papery label . . .

Then the doorbell rang, and when Tinkerbell dashed past them to open the door, there stood Cloudier-Klaudia, leaning heavily on a pair of crutches.

'Duh!' she said. 'Red front door! How did I forget that?'

'Um . . . Hello again!' said Clover, guiltily flipping the bag closed.

Pea hastily did up the buckles while Klaudia levered herself into the hallway.

She was wearing the same jeans as yesterday, only now one leg flapped open. Underneath, her left leg was in a plaster cast up to her knee, with hard purple webbing wound around it and her bare toes poking out at the bottom. Pea could see her shoe sticking out of her yellow coat pocket. The other pocket bulged with something furry, and what looked like green twigs.

'Oh yeah!' said Klaudia, following Pea's gaze and plunging her hand awkwardly into the pocket. She pulled out a fluffy blue teddy bear with GET WELL SOON printed on its tummy, and a bunch of pink carnations, rather squashed. 'Here!' she said, thrusting the flowers at Mum. 'To say thanks. Sorry they're so totally horrible. And this is for the doggie.' She threw the bear to Tinkerbell, who beamed.

'So your ankle was broken, then?' said Clover.

'Wuffly's was too,' said Tinkerbell. 'She had to have an operation. She's OK, though; just a bit sleepy.'

'I think Klaudia knows the feeling.' Mum quickly put out an arm as Klaudia swayed on her feet. 'Come in, my lovely. Can you manage? Are you supposed to be up and about?'

With a bit of help from Mum, Klaudia stumped into the front room and flopped down onto the Hannah Montana inflatable sofa.

'Oof,' she said, stretching out her leg while Mum went off to make cups of tea. 'Sorry. They gave me some tablets this morning, and they made me go *completely* lala. I got in a taxi and I'd, like, totally forgotten I'd spent all my money in the gift shop. And I couldn't remember the name of this road. Worst passenger ever! The taxi bloke was awesome, though. He just drove me up and down, knocking on doors till we got the right one. I met some dead nice people. An old man gave me a cake because he said he liked my hair. And a girl down the road said she'd knit me a sock to go over my toes, so they don't go blue and fall off.'

Pea nodded understandingly. That was exactly the sort of thing that happened to Mum. Whenever she needed help, suddenly people would appear to volunteer exactly what was required – lifts in their car, or a shoe that didn't have one heel falling off, or a place to live for a few months. Pea had always assumed it was some special Mummifying mermaidish charm she had. Klaudia wasn't at all mermaidish or Mum-like, but Pea liked her all the same.

'Didn't your family come to pick you up from the hospital?' asked Tinkerbell, stroking Wuffly's ears while she snored on the floor.

Klaudia shook her head. 'I'm from Germany. My family are all in Düsseldorf.'

She said *Düsseldorf* in a different voice from her ordinary one, as if she were switching over to being a different person.

'We used to live in Germany!' said Clover.

'*Wirklich? Und wo? Ich war so lange nicht mehr dort . . .*' said Klaudia brightly, in that other person's voice again.

'Oh,' said Clover. 'Sorry. It was years and years ago, and we weren't there for very long. I only really remember *Das ist eine Banane.*'

'And *Ich mag keinen joghurt,*' added Pea feelingly. (They had lived in a commune that was very keen on yogurt for breakfast. Pea hadn't liked it at all.)

Klaudia grinned. 'Ha! That's OK. I only really lived in Germany until I was six. Then Vati – he's an economic correspondent for newspapers – he moved us to Johannesburg, then Mumbai, Hong Kong, London—'

'That's just like us!' said Clover. 'We've lived all over the world. Goa, Norway, Prestatyn. Pea was born on a Greek island.'

'It's true.' Pea felt very exotic and special as Klaudia whistled, clearly impressed. 'I don't remember it, because I was only just born and Mum left not very long afterwards. But I expect I'll go there one day, to see what it's like.'

'Pretty cool,' said Klaudia. 'I love travelling. I adore London, though. I was here at school when I was around your age. I'm a grad student now, at Chelsea Art College.'

'Really?' said Mum, bringing in a heavy tray of mugs. 'Oh, you lucky thing. I always wanted to go to art college.'

'Did you?' asked Pea, shocked.

That wasn't what it said on Mum's website. It said: *Marina Cove never wanted to be anything but a writer*. Pea had written that bit herself.

'Ooh, yes,' said Mum, looking dreamily off into space. 'I was ever so arty at school. That's what I would've done at uni – but then I had Clover and, well, a baby changes all your plans when you're only eighteen.'

'I didn't know that,' said Clover, in a small voice. 'That I changed all your plans.'

Mum tucked a lock of wavy blonde hair

behind Clover's ear and kissed her forehead. 'You were a lovely surprise, and if I had my time over I wouldn't do a thing differently. All right?'

Clover nodded and sipped her tea, but a little crinkle of guilty worry stayed between her eyes. Pea rubbed her own forehead and found one there too.

'So do you live in halls at the college, then, Klaudia?' asked Mum. 'That must be so much fun. All those wild student parties . . . intellectual late-night discussions . . .'

Klaudia pulled a face. 'Hum, not exactly,' she said. 'I've been renting a room off this guy, but I sort of got a bit behind with the rent, so he threw me out. That's why I had all my stuff on the bike.'

'And where were you going?'

'Dunno,' giggled Klaudia. 'Was still figuring that out when . . .' She made a *Crkkk!* noise and pointed at her leg.

Tinkerbell stiffened, and put her hands over Wuffly's ears, just in case.

'You mean – you're a tragic penniless artist?' said Clover, in a whisper.

'Ha! Yep!'

Pea couldn't understand why Klaudia was laughing. There was nothing funny about being homeless. But Klaudia ran her fingers through her leopard-printed hair, and her eyes twinkled.

'Life should be full of unexpected things,' she said. 'Something'll turn up. All I need is to find someone who has an empty room in their house for a few months.'

'Well, we've got one of those,' said Clover. Then she visibly thought about it, gasped, and stared meaningfully at Mum.

'Oh, Clover – that's lovely, but, well, our spare room's for the new Vitória,' Mum explained. 'The au pair. Our last one left, so we need a new one quite urgently. If you know anyone who's looking for work . . . ?'

'I could do it,' said Klaudia.

'Oh, no, not on top of an art degree! It's a lot

of hours, and nothing glamorous. Shouting at Tinkerbell. Cleaning the loo.'

'I could do those.'

'With a broken leg?'

'Sure!'

'If you lived with us, would you draw pictures of me, Klaudia?' asked Clover.

'Hum, well, I'm not that sort of artist, really – I do, like, installations, conceptual work, you know? – but okey-dokey, why not?'

'Would you let me borrow your crutches?' said Tinkerbell.

'Sure!'

'Have you worked with children before, Klaudia?' said Mum, looking anxious.

Klaudia shook her head. 'Never. But I've worked with a lot with people, and children are people, right? Only newer.'

'See? That's the sort of thing *you* say, Mum. She's perfect,' said Clover. 'Isn't she perfect?'

Tinkerbell nodded firmly.

They both looked at Pea.

'Anything you wanted to ask, Pea-pod?' said Mum.

'Um,' said Pea. 'Yes. What *is* in your black canvas bag?'

'Ha! Something *very* precious,' Klaudia chuckled, then beckoned for her to fetch it.

Once Pea had placed the bag at her feet, Klaudia leaned down with a wince and a groan, and unbuckled it, folding back the flap and reaching inside to pull out . . .

A tin of paint.

'Oh,' said Pea, trying not to sound too disappointed.

'No-no-no.' Klaudia grinned. 'See, you think this is, like, just an ordinary tin of paint, yeah? But you're wrong.' She bent forward and lowered her voice – and they all leaned closer to hear. 'Inside this tin is a paint of a colour no one has ever seen before.'

'Whoa,' said Tinkerbell.

'Really?' said Clover.

Pea didn't say anything. Instead she let the idea roll around in her head, trying to picture what an entirely new colour might look like.

'*But!*' said Klaudia loudly, making them all jump. 'Before you ask – nope, I can't open the tin. Because if I show you, it would no longer be a colour no one had ever seen before. It must remain a mystery.'

'But what does it *look* like?' insisted Tinkerbell.

'Think of blue,' said Klaudia. 'Now think of the opposite. That's it exactly. But brighter.'

'Does it have a name?' Pea asked.

'*Klaudia*, of course!'

Pea tried really very hard to picture the colour of Klaudia – but her head wouldn't come up with new colours, only the familiar old ones. Tinkerbell and Clover's faces were crumpled with the same concentration. But Mum was watching with a broad, warm smile on her lips.

'Right, you three,' she said. 'Go away and be

quiet and lovely for at least ten minutes, so as not to put Klaudia off. We need to talk about grown-up stuff like money, and I should be sensible and check whether the poor thing has any idea at all how horrible three children can be.'

They all trooped off to the kitchen.

Tinkerbell put chocolate biscuits on a plate (she tested one on the way, which meant they each got to have one so it was fair). Clover put some grapes next to the biscuits, 'So it looks like we're healthy.' Then, after a suitable wait, they carried the tray back to the front room and knocked.

'Shhh,' said Mum, opening the door a crack.

Inside, Klaudia was lying on the inflatable sofa, her head tipped back and soft snorty snores coming out of her open mouth.

'I think the hospital tablets made her a bit sleepy,' whispered Mum. 'But she said yes! Congratulations, my swans. We've found a new Vitória by accident!'

CHAPTER 3

BACK TO SCHOOL

Dear Clem,
Happy New Year! I hope you had a nice party.
Here is all our New Year news:

• We were supposed to go to the Paget-
Skidelskys' next door but Mum was worried
about Wuffly getting lonely, so they had half
of their party at our house first. I had risotto
balls and 'wine' (grape juice).

• London people stay up really late and sing

outside in drunk voices for New Year's Eve, just like in Tenby.

• I expect Mum told you we've got a new Vitória called Klaudia (but you say it like Cloudier because she's a bit German). She has purple hair and is very brilliant and artistic. And sleepy.

• Clover's New Year's resolution is to be 'more serene', because she got a necklace with *Serenity* written in gold for Christmas. We shall see.

• Tink's New Year's resolution was to have her eighth birthday now instead of in May so she can join the Kensal Rise Kites like Sam Two, but Mum says that isn't the sort of thing you get to be resolved about.

• My New Year's resolution is to write three more *Girl Called Sky* stories and become a published author like Mum. (Sam One is going to do the covers and be a published-author-cover-maker – that's his resolution.)

• I don't know what Mum's and Klaudia's are.

Come and visit us again soon? We all liked you
staying at Christmas (even though the surprise
went a bit wrong).

Lots of love from Pea xx

---

3 January

Dear Diary,
I love Klaudia!
    Mum got in a panic because she has to
do a lecture about 'The Mermaid in Children's
Literature: 1910 to the Present Day' to some
librarians, so she was banished to the study and
we had to do all the house things. But because
Klaudia was in charge, we only did the fun ones,
like cleaning the kitchen floor by covering it in
squirty lemon stuff then skiing across it on old
tea towels. Then we went to Tesco, and we didn't

even have a list. Klaudia sat inside the trolley with her plaster-leg hanging out, and made us push her around really fast while shouting 'Kit Kats!' and pointing madly at the biscuit aisle. Vitória would NEVER have let us do that.

I've forgotten to be sad that it isn't Christmas any more for nearly two whole days.

4 January

Dear Diary,
Today we had toast IN BED for breakfast. With JAM.

Then Sam One came over and we worked out the next bit of *A Girl Called Sky*. (There is a plague of ants on her planet and Sam One has drawn ants crawling all over the pages as if they are crawling out of the story.) Sam Two was supposed to come over as well, but she was busy with football practice so Tink sat on the stairs outside my bedroom making 'huff' noises till we let her help. She's not very good at ants, but we didn't want to be mean. It's hard being a big sister. (Unless you are Clover, who did door-slamming. I am not at all sure that counts as serene.)

There is jam on my pillow. Oh well.

---

5 January

Dear Diary,

Today Klaudia drew portraits of us all! Tink wouldn't sit still but Klaudia said it didn't matter for her sort of art – which is true, because when she was finished, Tink had a head shaped like a wonky rectangle with levers and dials instead of a face. My portrait was sort of the same only she tore the paper to make my head into a cloud, and my eyes were made out of the letter 'a' from the fridge magnets and a wet splodge from her finger dipped in tea. Then she drew Clover, who was still being all cross and grumpy – only that portrait was a real one, all sketchy lines of pencil. It looks *exactly* like Clover, only more beautiful.

I don't know why Klaudia would draw things all modern and weird when she's so good at proper drawing. But Sam One says it's an artist

thing. I expect it's like when people ask why Mum writes about mermaids instead of famines, divorces, etc. If you are doing creativity, you

have to do what you like, and not mind about sniffy people.

I wonder what my hair would look like if I cut it very short and made it look leopard-printy?

Klaudia was certainly nothing like a real au pair.

While it was New Year and still felt holidayish, that meant lots of fun. But when everyone over-slept until nine minutes past eight on the first day of the new school term, panic set in.

'You can't be cross with Klaudia, Mum,' said Tinkerbell as Mum flung open kitchen cupboards,

54

hunting for something that wasn't the Kit Kats and Pot Noodles they'd sneaked into Klaudia's shopping trolley, while frantically ironing new creases into their crumpled school uniforms with her other hand. 'She's just like you.'

'Exactly!' wailed Mum. 'This family's already got one incompetent adult; we didn't need another one.'

'But she's allowed to make mistakes, she's new!' said Pea as a loud snore emerged from Klaudia's bedroom.

'*And* she's got a broken leg,' said Tinkerbell.

'*And* she's going to draw me again tonight,' said Clover. 'She says she likes my cheekbones. I've always thought they were good ones, but it's different when an artist says so, isn't it? Please don't send her away, Mum. She'd be homeless. Imagine: a homeless, one-legged artist . . . Oh, the cruelty . . .'

Pea and Clover exchanged desperate looks.

'I'm not going to send her away!' said Mum.

'And she's not one-legged! We'll have to have a little sit down together later, that's all, and talk about rules. I should've done it before; it was silly to think she'd be just like Vitória.'

There was a silence.

Clover sighed wistfully, twisting strands of hair around her finger. 'Remember when Vitória did my hair all twirly?'

'And her fluffy yellow dressing gown?' said Pea.

'And how she didn't mind me putting spiders in her bed?' said Tinkerbell.

'I know, my starlings, I miss her too,' said Mum.

Pea was stricken with a wave of guilt for all her diary entries, which had barely mentioned Vitória – when only a few weeks ago she'd been like part of the family. She ran upstairs at once, and put on the 'P' necklace Vitória had given her before she left.

Mum threw her warm winter coat and boots on over her pyjamas and steered an unimpressed Tinkerbell to the front door. Pea and Clover quickly got dressed, and picked up naughty flapjacks for breakfast from the shop by the bus stop. Pea spent the journey on the top deck of the bus, taking small bites of flapjack and writing a heartfelt (but rather wobbly) letter to Vitória.

Dear Vitória,

We miss you an awful lot, and definitely haven't forgotten you or anything like that. We have a Klaudia to look after us now, and even though she's fun and has leopard-printed hair, we still totally miss you and wish you were here.

Lots and lots and lots of love,
Pea xx (and everyone else)

'Is it all right?' asked Pea.

Clover licked her treacly fingers, then took the pen and added:

P.S. I hope it's sunny in Brazil! Send us photos. Cx

'That way she'll write back,' said Clover confidently. 'Maybe she can send Klaudia twirly-hairdo
instructions? We're going to have Drama Club
auditions this week, and I always act better with
twirly hair.'

By the time they got to the gates of Greyhope's,
Pea was feeling much better. This was exactly what
she needed: the comfy, familiar routine of school.

Clover was enveloped by a throng of younger
Drama Club girls, all desperate to find out if she
knew what production they'd be doing this term.
Pea hurried in out of the cold to her form room,
where everyone was talking about their Christmas
presents.

'I got a double duvet set with horses on it,' said
Pea's friend Bethany.

'CDs!' shouted Eloise, who seemed to have
grown taller and even more chesty, but apparently
still went everywhere with her earbud headphones
playing very loud music.

'I got a few different things,' said Molly, who

was wearing brand-new glasses with thin black frames instead of her old round red ones, and looking very self-conscious about it.

'I like your new glasses,' said Pea. 'I got lots of different things too, but this is my favourite.'

She showed them the 'P' necklace (they weren't really allowed jewellery at school, but it tucked under her shirt easily enough). Then she told them all about the accident, and Wuffly's leg, and Klaudia, all of which sounded much more exciting than Christmas.

By mid-morning Pea was feeling quite at home again. The next lesson was English, with Mrs Embury. They hadn't been given any holiday homework, but Pea had printed off a copy of *A Girl Called Sky* for her to read, with bubble letters for the title across the top and some of Sam One's illustrations scanned in. The *Spark!* magazine website *still* hadn't revealed its Young Writers' Award winners yet, but it was sure to, any day now. Pea had always been quiet so as not to be in the way in

English lessons last term, but she was certain Mrs Embury would like to see the story before it was famous. But Mrs Embury was not at her desk.

Instead, there was a man with longish dark hair, an earring and a faint scruff of beard sitting at the front of the classroom, tutting over last term's exercise books. All the tables were now in straight lines facing forward, instead of in groups. The walls, which had been covered with things to look at – Year Ten's war poems, and a cardboard Shakespeare with ideas in clouds over his head – were now blank and bare, with lots of little holes where staples had been pulled out. Pea and Bethany moved to sit at the furthest away seats possible, right at the back – but on every table there was a small folded card with each student's name. Bethany was two rows back; Pea was in the front row – listed as *Prudence*. She slipped the card into her pocket before anyone else could see it.

Gradually the rest of the class arrived, all looking as confused as Pea.

'Places are allocated – *don't* move them around, please,' said the man, still not looking up.

Molly came to sit on one side of her, and Lilly (who didn't like Pea at all) on the other.

'My name is Mr Ellis,' said the new teacher eventually, writing *MR ELLIS* on the board in towering, jagged red-marker-pen capitals. 'Mrs Embury will no longer be teaching at this school. Which, judging by the state of your work from last term, is a very good thing.' He lifted the pile of exercise books and dropped them all in the bin with a *thunk*.

Pea and Molly shared a look of horror. Last term, all Pea's work had come back with a cheerful *Good!* or *A fine effort!* written beneath it in green biro, sometimes with a smiley face and a house point. And now it was in the bin.

'To allow me to confirm exactly how far behind acceptable standards you have fallen, we will begin with a written test.'

Pea's heart sank. Normally the teacher would

61

tell you if there was going to be a test, so you could lie awake the night before worrying about it.

'It'll be all right, you're good at English,' Molly whispered.

But the next hour was spent on a bewildering series of questions. First, they had to underline the *subject* and the *object* in twelve sentences. (Pea didn't have a clue – Mrs Embury's lessons had never required any underlining, except the title at the top of a page so it looked nice – but she worked out that if she underlined different sorts of words in each sentence, then at least one or two of them had to be right.) There was a section for comparisons, like '*Ship* is to *Quay* as *Hospital* is to . . . ?' which made no sense at all. There was a comprehension test, with a long confusing paragraph about a man arriving at a house in the middle of a storm – but the questions had multiple-choice answers, and in every single one, Pea thought neither A nor B nor C nor D was the right answer. Finally, examples of *the passive voice* were to be identified in another long confusing paragraph.

Mr Ellis told them to swap papers with a neighbour, and they marked them right away, with him reading out the answers. Lilly put large, enthusiastic crosses next to all Pea's mistakes. At the end, Molly had scored 19 out of 50. Lilly got 24.

Pea's paper came back with *6 out of 50* written at the bottom.

'Oh dear,' said Mr Ellis, plucking the test out of her hands as he stalked around the room.

'I hate him,' said Bethany feelingly, once they were safely out of the classroom.

'Me too,' whispered Molly.

Pea was too devastated to say anything, but she didn't need to: they all understood. English was Pea's best subject, always. It said that writing was one of her special skills on her CV. She was going to be a writer, like Mum, when she grew up. Could you be a writer if you only got 6 out of 50 in an English test?

Bethany shared her Wotsits at lunch time to

cheer Pea up, but she was still worrying about it when she and Clover got home. Usually Mum was very quick to spot a droopy pair of shoulders, but not today. She was wearing her comfy trackie bottoms and pencils in her hair, a sure sign that her mind was full of mermaids, and was sitting at the kitchen table surrounded by empty tea mugs and scribbled-on sheets of paper.

'The blank page, yeah,' Klaudia was saying in a sympathetic voice. 'Scary. But, like, exciting, you know?'

'*Yeah*,' said Mum, nodding a lot.

'*Yeah*,' said Klaudia. 'Like, my project for this term is going to be a self-portrait. One single artwork that encapsulates my entire life experience, for the Student Showcase. Only, I think every piece of art I make is a self-portrait – you know what I mean?'

'Yeah!' said Mum, thumping the table. 'Exactly!'

'Hey, you mind if I start on the self-portrait here in the house, though? Like, make my room into a little studio? With my leg it's a pain to go to college every day. It'll be all done by the end of March. And that way I'll be around more for the girls.'

'Of course!' Mum's eyes were sparkly with glee. 'We can work together! Oh, it's so lovely to have another creative person in the house. Art college sounds such *fun*. All that time and space to just . . . make stuff. Don't you think so, girls? How was school, my pets?'

'Fine,' yawned Clover. 'Drama Club auditions aren't till Friday, so nothing important happened.'

'Um,' said Pea. 'I've got a new English teacher. Mr Ellis.'

'Oh, I've got him too,' said Clover, suddenly perking up. 'He's *gorgeous*. He's got man-jewellery and big blue eyes, and he's ever so stern. All of Year Nine are completely in love with him already.'

Pea opened her mouth, then closed it again. How could anyone be in love with Mr Ellis? Clover wouldn't be once she heard all about the awful test

– but suddenly the words 'six out of fifty' sounded too terrible to repeat.

'I'll just go and check on Wuffly,' she mumbled, and fled.

The next morning Mum pinned a *Plan for the Week* to the fridge above their CVs, and Klaudia stuck to it beautifully. She reminded them to brush their teeth before bed, switched off the TV instead of being the one who turned it on, and even – to Tinkerbell's disgust – created a household rota of tasks that the sisters should do to help her out, just as Vitória had done.

She still had to rest her leg a lot, and take special pills, which meant she nodded off at unfortunate moments. She still laughed when Wuffly tried to stand up and fell over her broken leg, instead of making soothing noises. One evening she was so busy drawing another sketch of Clover, she failed to notice that the kitchen was ever so slightly on fire. But when she discovered the source (Tinkerbell, putting Kit Kat wrappers in the toaster to see if they'd make sparks), Klaudia sent her to her room at once, very severely, without even a trace of a giggle.

The rest of Pea's first week back at school, however, went as badly as the first day. Clover had been right: Mr Ellis's door always seemed to be surrounded by Year Nine girls, whispering behind their hands whenever he walked past and dissolving into pink-faced giggles if he spoke to them. Not Pea. She had English every day, and every day Mr Ellis would come up with a new way to make her feel intensely dim. On Tuesday it was Comprehension Exercises. Wednesday, they had Grammar. On Thursday they did Extended Writing – non-fiction, with a list of required words to include, like *speculate* and *participatory*, that made what she was writing have to bend itself all out of shape to fit them in. Friday brought the worst of all: Oral Presentations.

'You will each give a one-minute speech to the

class on the topic provided,' said Mr Ellis on Friday afternoon, handing round a box filled with folded slips of paper. 'You are not expected to be an expert on that topic. I will simply be assessing your ability to speak clearly, with confidence, in language appropriate for your audience. You will each be given a mark out of five – five being the highest.'

A series of gasps and moans rippled across the rows, cut short at once by a glare from Mr Ellis. Pea felt perfectly sick. Standing up and talking in front of other people was what Clover was good at – so Pea had never really needed to learn.

Pea's slip of paper said OWLS.

She turned it over in case it said something else on the back, but it didn't.

One minute. On owls. In front of the whole class.

Pea felt even sicker.

She tried frantically to remember anything at all about owls while the first few names were called.

Shruti Cox-Patel stood up and spoke, incredibly quickly, about 'Television' and how it was the cause of brain decay and eye damage and was the very worst invention of all time – which Pea thought was strange, since on Monday she'd overheard Shruti telling everyone about the huge widescreen TV she'd got for Christmas, but still, it seemed like the sort of thing you were meant to say at school. Being in the front row, Pea could see the book with everyone's names open on Mr Ellis's desk, and Shruti got a 3.

Molly had to make a loud speech about 'Food', which veered from the horribleness of McDonald's and the tragic fate of poor cows that hadn't done any harm to anyone, to how much she liked lasagne. She got a 2.

After what seemed like hours of 'Role Models' and 'War', it was Pea's turn. She stood up, staring at the slip of paper that said OWLS as if it might suddenly turn into a speech she could read. Her mind was a blank.

'Owls,' said Pea.

'Louder!' barked Mr Ellis.

'Owls,' she said again, trying to make her voice big. 'Owls is my topic, so I am going to talk to you about Owls. Which are birds. That fly at night-time.'

That really was all Pea knew about Owls, but Mr Ellis cleared his throat and looked very pointedly at his stopwatch.

'Oh,' said Pea brightly, remembering they were in an English lesson, 'and in *Harry Potter* they bring letters, so they're sort of like postmen, or postwomen, only they're pets as well. And there's a picture book called *Owl Babies*, and it made my mum cry when she read it to us as a bedtime story even though the ending's happy.'

Beside her, Lilly snorted out loud.

'I mean, when she used to read it when we were little!' Pea protested.

Lilly snorted again. Mr Ellis went on looking pointedly at his stopwatch.

'Um. And . . . Owls are birds, and they fly at night . . . Oh, and they eat mice!' Pea added quickly, half remembering an old class project from Tenby primary. 'They swallow their food whole, so sometimes you find whole mouse skeletons in their . . .' She didn't think you were supposed to say 'poo' in an Oral Presentation, so she had to stop dead in the middle of her sentence. By that point Mr Ellis had already shouted 'Speak up!' and 'Can't hear you!' several more times, so she kept her lips moving and hoped that he'd think she was still speaking, only very quietly, until the time ran out.

Mr Ellis gave her a 0.

Once everyone else had stumbled through their miserable short speeches on 'The Sea' and 'Newspapers', Mr Ellis announced that they would be doing Oral Presentations on random days every week for the rest of term, until they got less terrible at it.

'Mr Ellis did the same with us,' said Clover gloomily on the bus home. 'I had to talk about "Tragedy", so of course I told him all about having a dead dad – and *Hamlet*, a bit. Maybe you should join Drama Club, Pea – that'll help you get used to standing up and talking with everyone looking at you. Mrs Sharma says she's going to be giving the main parts to all sorts of random people this term. She says it's not fair if only one person is always in the spotlight – even if I *am* the most talented. She didn't say that last part, but she was definitely thinking it.' Clover's lips scrunched together, as if she might want to say something extremely un-serene about Mrs Sharma's new casting policy.

The moment they got home, Clover thudded upstairs and put on *100 Songs from Stage and Screen*, extra-loud.

It was no use Pea trying to talk to Mum or Klaudia: they were busy chopping up a huge pile of mushrooms (Dr Skidelsky spent weekdays working in Edinburgh, and Dr Paget had gone to meet her train, so the Sams were staying for dinner) and were lost in conversation about some famous painting of a scream.

Tinkerbell was outside playing football, even though it was drizzly and cold and almost completely dark. Pea could hear her breathlessly shouting, 'Look, Sam, look, I've been practising, look,' through the kitchen window, although Sam Two was watching TV in the front room.

But Sam One was happy to listen to Pea's worries.

'Why does it matter how you do at school?' he said, floppy brown hair falling over his nose as he coloured in another space ant crawling across *A Girl Called Sky*.

'Because . . .' said Pea. 'Because it's *school*. It's where people decide what you're good at. Imagine if your teacher told you that you weren't any good at art – what would you do then?'

'But she wouldn't.'

'What if she did?'

Sam One frowned, and chewed his coloured pencil. 'Well,' he said eventually, 'I'd know she was wrong, so it wouldn't matter.' And he carried on colouring his space ant. His good, really undeniably good, space ant.

It was so simple, yet so reassuring. Teachers could be wrong. Pea went to sleep feeling calm, and dreamed that next week at school Mr Ellis was replaced by Miss Honey from *Matilda*, who cancelled Oral Presentations at once. But Saturday dragged by slowly. It rained and rained, and Pea spent much of the day curled up with Wuffly, stroking her ears and feeding her crumbs from the last of her Christmas treats bag. Wuffly looked very mournful, lying awkwardly on one side with her plaster cast sticking out stiffly. Every now and then she would get licky, and her eyes would brighten up, and she would try to bound onto her paws and go skittering down the hall like always – only to remember her poorly leg, and flop back onto her old blue blanket. Pea knew exactly how she felt. Her mind would drift away quite happily as she listened to Tinkerbell trying to persuade Klaudia to draw rabbit ears on the sketch of Clover. Then, suddenly, she would feel a plunging sensation of gloom, and it would all flood back.

What if Mr Ellis wasn't wrong?

6 out of 50.

0 out of 5.

Each time she caught sight of her CV still pinned up on the fridge, proudly declaring *writing* and *reading* under her *Special skills*, and *writer (like Mum)* under *Future career*, she felt her face grow pink with shame.

'Hey, Pea! You've got an email!' called Clover, just before bedtime.

Pea walked dejectedly into the study, where Clover was googling 'serenity' in her pyjamas at Mum's lamplit desk, surrounded by a mess of Post-it notes for the new *Mermaid Girls* book.

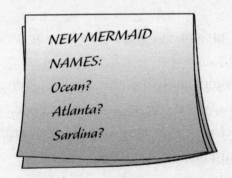

NEW MERMAID
NAMES:
Ocean?
Atlanta?
Sardina?

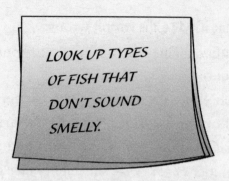

LOOK UP TYPES
OF FISH THAT
DON'T SOUND
SMELLY.

Mum's computer screen glowed in the darkness.

There, in front of her, was a new message, from *Spark!* magazine, headed WINNER!!!

Clover's eyes shone in the lamplight. 'Well, go on, open it!' she said excitedly, shifting off the chair so Pea could sit down.

Pea's finger hovered over the mouse and clicked.

The ancient computer loaded the new page, agonizingly slowly.

Pea could barely breathe. Mr Ellis didn't matter now. This was it, the moment she'd been waiting for: her chance to become a published author, just like Mum . . .

CONGRATULATIONS!
to Adeola Vincent, winner of our Young
Writers' Award!
You can read her incredible tale of star-
crossed lovers, *Kiss Me, Kyril*, right now on the
Spark! website.

There was a photograph of a grinning girl around Clover's age holding up a page from her story in front of a snowy Christmas tree. They must have taken it ages ago. All this time Pea had been waiting and hoping, and the *Spark!* website people had known all along that she hadn't won.

'Oh, *Pea*,' said Clover, squeezing her shoulder.

Pea tried clutching her thumbs, but it didn't stop a few tears rolling down her cheeks. The moment she saw them, Clover began to sniffle too.

'What are you all weeping about now?' said Tinkerbell, peering in on her way back from pinching a biscuit out of the tin.

'Everything's gone horrible,' sighed Clover, and

77

she explained about Pea's writing competition, and about Mrs Sharma thinking other people ought to be allowed parts in plays.

Tinkerbell patted Pea's other shoulder sympathetically. 'I bet that Adeola person's story is rubbish compared to yours,' she said helpfully, and offered Pea her half-eaten biscuit.

Miserably, Pea clicked through to the winning story.

It was about a girl who was a werewolf and a boy who was a ghost. There were lots of descriptions of their faces, and how much she wanted to kiss his eyebrows in the moonlight. It wasn't the sort of story Pea liked much. People in those kinds of books always listened to bands she'd never heard of, and were unhappy all the time, even though they never had to do Oral Presentations about Owls. But there was a sinister shadowy figure following the werewolf and the ghost around, and they had to read all the way to the end to find out who it was – all three leaning closer and closer to the screen as the story got more exciting – which was probably a sign that it was quite good. And Pea would never have guessed that the sinister shadowy figure was the boy all along – who wasn't a ghost yet, because of time-travel – and at the end the girl turned into a werewolf and killed him by mistake – which was quite clever when you thought about it.

Even Pea had to admit they'd chosen a good winner.

'She's a bit older than you,' said Tinkerbell. 'That's probably the main reason why she won.'

'No, it's not.' Pea sniffed and, in a very quiet voice, admitted the awful 6 out of 50. 'So you see, I don't think I'm cut out to be a writer. Not really.'

Tinkerbell looked shocked. Clover did too – but only for a moment. She lifted her chin, snatched a pencil off Mum's desk and marched to the kitchen. Pea and Tinkerbell followed, and the three of them lined up in front of the CVs on the fridge.

To Pea's astonishment, Clover drew a firm line through *actor/director of plays* on her CV beside

79

Future career, and replaced it with a large question mark.

'But you've always done acting!' said Tinkerbell.

'Is this because of Drama Club?' asked Pea.

Clover shook her tumbly blonde waves, though her face turned faintly pink. 'Not only that. Remember Mum told Klaudia she wanted to be an artist when she was younger? She changed her mind, and she's happy. Maybe none of us are supposed to be what we expect.'

Tinkerbell grinned and grabbed the pencil.

'Yours already says *yet to be determined*!' said Clover.

'I know, but I want a question mark like yours,' said Tinkerbell, crossing it out anyway.

Tinkerbell passed the pencil to Pea. Pea looked at it numbly, then slowly lifted it to the page.

'Are you sure?' whispered Clover.

Pea nodded.

'But what will you be instead?' asked Tinkerbell.

Pea looked at the empty space next to *Future*

career, thought for a moment, and then, with her pencil, crossed out *writer (like Mum)* and added her own very big '?'.

PEA

Age: 11

Current occupation: schoolgirl

Likes: books

Special skills: writing, reading, making sandwiches

Future career: ~~writer (like Mum)~~ ?

CHAPTER 4

A NEW PEA

Now that Pea's Sunday was not taken up with dreaming of Sky and whether the moon was made of cheese, there seemed to be a lot of it. Usually when she was bored, she would read. But reading wasn't fun any more. Even the *Mermaid Girls* books didn't tempt her.

Once upon a time she had held each of them reverently, imagining her own name on the spine, and a gorgeous photograph of herself looking wistful and intelligent on the back flap, just like Mum's.

Pea Llewellyn never wanted to be anything other than a writer. The daughter of a successful novelist and an absentee pirate, she was always destined to live in a fantasy world. She published her first book aged 12. She is now famous all around the world and everyone thinks she's really brilliant.

It had been such a long-held dream it was hard to let it go, but now, under her wistful intelligent face, all she could picture was:

Pea Llewellyn once got 6 out of 50 on an English test, and, what with the internet, no one cares much about books and stories these days anyway . . .

in jagged red marker pen.

The '?' at the end of her CV loomed ominously from the fridge door every time she ventured near the kitchen. But what could a Pea be, if not a writer?

'It's very liberating, not being tied to acting any more,' said Clover airily on the Monday morning bus to school. 'Honey and Tash invited me for coffee and shops loads of times last term, but I always had rehearsals, or lines to learn. My life's going to be so exciting now.'

'It feels a bit scary to me,' confessed Pea.

'Well, what would you *like* to be,' said Clover, 'now that you can pick absolutely anything, out of all the billions of jobs in the world?'

Pea's nose wrinkled up with indecision (not that Clover noticed; she had her eyes serenely shut, and was humming). 'That's the problem,' she whispered, looking around at all the people on the bus dressed up in office-y clothes, going off to do who knew what. 'I don't really understand what most grown-ups *do*.'

Tinkerbell's dad Clem was an estate agent. Klaudia was a student and an au pair. And after that her mind skipped to astronauts and princesses, none of whom seemed likely to be wearing a tie or clicky high heels on the bus.

Pea's friends were much more helpful.

Bethany's parents both did 'something in IT'. Molly's mum was the managing director of a chain of fashion shops. Eloise's dad and stepmum ran a catering company which made food for weddings and really big birthday parties – but none of them planned to do what their parents did.

'I'm going to train horses,' said Bethany.

'Bass player in a band,' said Eloise.

'I was going to be a science teacher,' said Molly, quivering as they stepped into Mr Ellis's classroom and saw the word *TEST* written on the board. 'But I think I'd rather work in a lab now, as a molecular geneticist.'

If *they* all knew already what they wanted to do, Pea reasoned, it couldn't be that hard to find out who to be.

When she got home, she wrote out the options in her rainbow notebook, in order of preference:

THINGS TO BE:
IT (think this is computers – I am good at
those already)
Catering (making sandwiches; I like sandwiches)
Estate agent (Clem likes it)

THINGS NOT TO BE:
Molecular geneticist (hard to spell, don't know
what it is)
Managing director (sounds difficult)
Horse trainer (horses)
Bass player (Eloise says there are only four
strings so it's easy to learn, but you have to play
it in front of people on a stage)
Teacher (involves meanness to innocent children)

Feeling much more cheerful, Pea filled up her
evening tending to Wuffly, who was the saddest dog
in the world now that she had to wear a cone around

her head and couldn't do chasing. She would lie on her side, sighing and making hopeless whining noises in the middle of *Coronation Street*. Mum and Clover (who watched it together, compulsively eating toffees) shushed and complained, until Pea pulled the blue blanket – with Wuffly still sprawled on it – across the floor and out into the cool of the hallway.

Pea expected Tinkerbell to appear at once, and complain about Wuffly being dragged out to lie in the cold. But Tinkerbell was up in her bedroom. Now that she thought about it, Pea hadn't seen her tending to Wuffly much at all since the accident. Wuffly was the whole family's dog, but Tinkerbell's most of all (since she was the one who'd begged and pleaded with Clem for a puppy until he'd admitted defeat). Normally they were inseparable. But now that Wuffly wasn't a silly playful dog who skidded madly along the floor or could be instructed to bite nasty people on the ankle, Tinkerbell seemed to find her a bit boring.

Wuffly gave another mournful whine, as if she'd overheard Pea's thoughts.

'I know it's unkind,' Pea whispered, 'but she's only seven. She'll be your best friend again once you're all better.'

Wuffly licked Pea's palm, liquid brown eyes imploring her to . . . what? Mend her leg? Take off the cone?

'Shhhh,' said Pea, stroking her nose till she quieted. 'You're quite all right – you just need to be patient and wait for your leg to heal.'

Pea frowned. Only that morning, Klaudia had been sighing over not being able to ride her bike, or have a normal shower without sitting on the floor with one leg poking out; just ordinary things that you only noticed you missed when they were taken away. She gave Wuffly another pat before hurrying into the kitchen. She came back clutching Wuffly's favourite tatty ball, the one with the bell inside, and some photos off the pinboard of her bounding happily across Queen's Park.

Wuffly perked up at once.

She sniffed the photos, her tail wagging.

And when Pea batted the ball towards her, she barked, and batted it right back.

She tried to chase it too, in a three-legged run that ended with her nose-first in the umbrella bin – but Pea rescued ball and dog, and from then on kept the ball comfortably within reach. Once Wuffly had discovered she could catch high over-head throws in her cone, her tail beat the floor so hard Mum had to shut the door on them so she wouldn't interrupt Roy Cropper.

'Isn't she looking perkier!' said Mum, scruffling Wuffly's ears as the end theme music wailed into the hallway. 'Well done, Pea.'

Pea didn't think she'd done anything all that special. It was only rolling a ball about and giving Wuffly some photos to look at. But before she went to bed she put a hot-water bottle under the blue blanket, just to make sure the perkiness didn't fade. Wuffly shifted her hairy tummy onto the warm spot and gave a grateful whine.

The next evening, Pea did the same.

By the end of the week Wuffly had learned to shuffle on her belly up and down the hallway, and was waiting for Pea to come home from school, tail wagging, jingly ball at the ready.

'Hey, Tink, look at this!' called Pea, as Wuffly propelled herself after the ball with her one good back leg.

But Tinkerbell was in the garden playing football by herself, and could not be coaxed inside.

She was out there again on Saturday morning, before breakfast, in the pouring rain, trying to practise goal kicks while holding an umbrella. It was the day of Sam Two's first match for the Kensal Rise Kites. Since she couldn't be on the team, Tinkerbell had appointed herself head cheerleader. Klaudia had even helped her make some pompoms out of an old jumper and some glue.

To Tinkerbell's disgust, Pea and Clover declined the invitation to join her on the touchline.

It was just as well. The Paget-Skidelskys came round for lunch afterwards, bedraggled and rather sad. Tinkerbell's pompom glue had melted in the rain, and she returned clutching two fistfuls of soggy wool that dripped on the floor. Sam Two, meanwhile, looked as if she'd been in a swamp. Her trainers were brown all over, and there was a long streak of wet mud that went all the way up her left side, from her ankle to her nose. Even her ears were muddy.

'Did you win?' asked Mum, handing round towels.

Dr Paget winced. 'Fifteen–nil,' she mouthed, shaking her head.

'Sam played very well, though,' said Dr Skidelsky, her oblong glasses steaming up from the rain.

'I'd have played even better if we hadn't had to walk miles to get there,' said Sam Two sulkily.

'We got lost on the way,' said Dr Paget, wincing again. 'The Chalk Farm Chaffinches have their own minibus. And matching team socks. All rather embarrassing.'

Pea *had* expected to see Sam Two in a shiny football shirt with her name on the back, not trackie bottoms and a fleecy top. She didn't even have proper football boots.

'Don't suppose you know anyone who could lend us a minibus, Klaudia?' said Dr Skidelsky. 'Or maybe sponsor the team?'

'Soz.' Klaudia shrugged. 'I only know arty people and they're always, like, totally skint.'

Sam Two was taken home to get changed, and they all sat down to eat comforting hot lasagne.

'I could get the Kites some money. We did a Sponsored Silence at school,' said Tinkerbell thoughtfully, between mouthfuls.

'Yeah, and you got disqualified after thirty seconds,' snorted Clover.

'Perhaps not a Sponsored Silence, exactly,' said Dr Skidelsky, 'but it's a thought. Some kind of fundraising to give the Kites a boost . . .'

'You're not on the team, Tink,' said Sam Two, rolling her eyes. 'I keep telling her.'

'We noticed,' said Dr Paget sharply, until Sam Two shuffled in her chair and mumbled an apology. 'Of course you can help with some fundraising, Tink. You're always full of bright ideas.'

'That's one way of putting it,' said Mum, who had spent part of the morning sweeping up broken lightbulb after Tinkerbell invented Indoor Bed-Football. 'But I suppose it is a good cause. Just don't rob a bank or anything, all right?'

Tinkerbell beamed. She hopped down from the table, grabbed a pencil, and went to the fridge to change her CV.

TINKERBELL
Future career: ~~criminal mastermind~~
~~yet to be determined~~ ?
funraisin

'Well, if we're making things official, I also have an announcement to make,' said Clover grandly. 'I've decided on a change of career too.'

She took the pencil and updated her CV as well.

CLOVER
Future career: ~~actor/director of plays~~ ?
model

'Not the fashion sort – well, not yet, who knows? But I'm going to be a model. For Klaudia's life-drawing class at the university.'

'An artists' model?' said Dr Paget. 'As in . . . *naked*?'

'No!' laughed Klaudia. 'With all her clothes on. It's not a class for drawing, like, bottoms. Well, not always. Only we're short of models, and Clover did enjoy it when I sketched her, so I thought . . . do you mind?'

Mum looked doubtful.

'Klaudia said you could come too,' said Clover quickly.

'It's a public evening class, on Monday, and I'm the teacher, so no one's going to tell you off.'

Klaudia grinned. 'Go on, come and play at being an art student.'

It was exactly the right thing to say. Mum went slightly fluttery, and the whole of pudding time was taken up with the grown-ups talking about lost dreams and portrait galleries.

Pea sat on the floor feeding Wuffly scraps of pastry, feeling flat. Usually she and Sam One would've huddled at the end of the table together planning the next part of the Sky story, but today he sat there working on a comic strip of his own called *Space Ant vs. the Monkey Mummy*.

She kept looking at the fridge and seeing the great big '?' looming under her name. Suddenly *Something in IT* sounded very dull next to *funraisin* and *model*. *Catering* would mean making lots of sandwiches and not getting to eat them. And Clem used to yawn a lot when he talked about being an estate agent.

Pea still had no idea at all what she might become. It was as if she didn't have a future to look forward to at all.

'You're very good with that dog,' said Dr Paget, passing down another plate of leftovers so Wuffly could nibble on more scraps.

'If I was forced to lie about while someone fed me apple pie, I'd be happy too,' said Mum.

'No,' said Dr Skidelsky, quite seriously. 'After a shock like an accident, animals are often very difficult, even with people they know well. It's impressive, how comfortable she is with you, Pea. You're a natural.'

Pea blushed scarlet as everyone turned to look at her.

'Someone did say you should be a medic, after the accident,' Clover remembered. 'You could be a vet, Pea!'

'Oh, I think Pea's planning to follow in my footsteps, aren't you, my twiglet?' said Mum, smiling.

'Actually, Mum, I've decided I'm not going to be a writer after all.'

Mum gave Pea's CV a closer look; Pea could see her forehead crinkle with surprise. But what Dr Skidelsky had said was swelling in her chest, and suddenly she felt quite certain.

'And, um . . . Actually, I think I might like to work with animals.'

'You have to do, like, amazing in all your exams to be a vet,' said Klaudia. 'A-grades in everything.'

'Oh,' said Pea, thinking of the dreaded Mr Ellis. That was *that* future spoiled too.

'It's a bit soon for Pea to worry about exam results,' said Dr Paget rapidly. 'You wouldn't need to be a vet to work with animals anyway, Pea, dear. You could work at a rescue shelter, or a monkey sanctuary. Train guide dogs for the blind. There are pet therapists too. Humans are animals, and we treat *their* feelings. No reason why we shouldn't give pets the same courtesy.'

'*Really?*' asked Pea. 'You mean, I could do what you do?'

When Dr Skidelsky was in Edinburgh, she

spent her weekdays teaching at the university and writing up research papers about family psychology – but Dr Paget treated patients on the golden plush sofas of their living room next door. Pea had always thought it sounded quite easy, just drinking tea while people cried at you.

'Hang on,' said Sam One, frowning. 'All your patients come and tell you what's wrong with them. So they're easy to fix. Dogs can't do that.'

'No,' said Dr Skidelsky, 'but they can still communicate. Look – when Wuffly puts her ears back like that and makes that little crooning sound . . .'

'It means she wants more apple pie!' said Clover.

'She wants more when she blinks or wags her tail, though,' Mum pointed out. 'That dog is a big old pie-hoover. You should see her licking the floor after breakfast. By the time that cast comes off, you're going to look like a planet with legs, aren't you, baby?'

Mum leaned in to feed Wuffly another corner

of pastry – but she tilted her head firmly away, then buried her nose in Pea's hands.

'I think that means *Please stop making personal comments about me, I've gone a bit self-conscious,*' said Pea.

'You know, I think you're right.' Dr Skidelsky regarded Pea thoughtfully. 'I told you: a natural. Animal psychology, that's the path for you. I've got a friend in Edinburgh researching the domestic behaviour patterns of pigeons. I'll get her to lend you some books, if you like.'

'Um. Would I still need all A-grades in my exams?' asked Pea.

'Shouldn't think so,' said Dr Paget.

'Would I have to talk to pigeons too?'

Dogs were nice, friendly things. Pea wasn't sure she wanted to talk to anything flappy or pecky or that could poo on the top of your head.

Dr Skidelsky shook her head. 'Oh, my friend says pigeons are a bit dim, really. Doubt you'd get much of a conversation. But she's an academic. I was imagining you'd mostly be dealing with pets – the sort of animals people love enough to care about their feelings. A lonely pony. A depressed cat. Not slugs and such.'

'That's not fair,' said Sam One. 'Slugs have feelings too. Probably.'

Pea thought he might be right, but she didn't much fancy staring at a slug and trying to work out what it was thinking.

'Of course, there are zoos as well,' said Dr Paget. 'You might have to teach a crocodile how to smile. Cheer up a chimpanzee.'

'Calm a llama!' said Klaudia.

'Make a giraffe laugh?' suggested Dr Paget.

Wuffly nipped at Pea's hand, and she realized that the plate of apple pie on the floor had been licked entirely clean. 'All gone,' she said.

Wuffly bared her teeth and growled.

'You've had more than me!' Pea told her. 'If you have any more, you'll get a poorly tummy, and you've already got a poorly leg.'

Wuffly looked mournfully at her plaster cast, then nosed meaningfully at the empty plate.

'No more pie!' said Pea, making a cutting motion with her hand and lifting the plate up onto the table, out of sight. 'Go to sleep, silly dog.'

Finally Wuffly gave a defeated little bark, laid her head on her paws, and shut her eyes. Within moments, her wagging tail fell still.

'Well, I think that seals it,' said Mum, with a tiny sigh. 'My Pea-nut's going to be Doctor Dolittle.'

Pea scrambled up, took the pencil, crossed out the big ominous '?', and wrote:

pet therapist

Just looking at it made her smile. She had a future now, after all.

That night, after Pea had brushed her teeth and combed her hair, she curled up under the covers and took out her spiral-bound diary.

Dear Diary,

For all these long years I have kept writing in you, as practice for being a writer. Mum said that was a good idea, but I still got 6 out of 50 on my English test so she must have been a bit wrong. Anyway, now I am going to train as a pet therapist, I will be busy learning about animals, so I won't have time for you any more. I hope you understand. It is not at all personal, Diary.

Love from Pea x

She shut the diary away in her bedside table, put down the pen and clicked off the lamp. The moment she closed her eyes, Dr Skidelsky's words started to roll around in her head. *Impressive. A natural.* It made her wriggle with excitement.

She was still wide awake, thinking about how you might calm a llama, when there was a tapping at her bedroom door.

'Hello?' she said, clicking the light back on.

Tinkerbell peeped in, dressed in footie pyjamas, her small face pinched with worry. 'Are you asleep?' she whispered. 'I need to ask you an important thing.'

Pea patted the bed.

Tinkerbell sat down cross-legged and said, very seriously, 'Pea, is it true? Can you *really* talk to Wuffly?'

Pea thought about it. 'Um. Sort of. I mean, it's not like we can have a conversation about shopping or homework. I can't translate barking. But I can understand a bit of what Wuffly's thinking. At least, I think so. Why?'

Tinkerbell crinkled up her nose as if she wasn't quite sure she should say.

'Ohhh . . .' Suddenly Pea was sure she knew exactly what was keeping Tinkerbell awake. 'I don't think Wuffly's cross with you, Tink,' she said gently. 'She understands that she can't go out and play in the park or the garden as usual, so she isn't as much fun. Though she would really like you to pay her a bit more attention, because her leg hurts sometimes, and when you aren't well it's nice to have your best friends around.'

Tinkerbell's eyes went very wide.

Pea bit her lip. She'd made all that up, really. Even though it seemed like what Wuffly *might* be thinking, or *ought* to be thinking, she didn't know for certain.

But Tinkerbell wasn't upset. In fact, she seemed delighted.

'Amazing,' she breathed, gazing at Pea with starry-eyed admiration. 'Perfect! Goodnight!'

And she hopped off the bed and down the little attic steps quite happily, leaving Pea feeling very confused.

PEA LLEWELLYN: DOG WHISPERER

Pea felt guilty when she woke up on Sunday morning. She hadn't meant for Tinkerbell to think she had magical dog-mind-reading powers. But, she consoled herself, at least it might make Tinkerbell a little bit more thoughtful.

But if anything, Tinkerbell was worse. At breakfast she ignored Wuffly completely, and kept her nose stuffed firmly in one of her school books, scribbling hard.

'Homework – don't interrupt!' she shouted if anyone asked.

Clover went off to Klaudia's room to practise art-worthy model poses. Mum went to the study to think of a new title for the as-yet-unwritten *Mermaid Girls 5*. (Apparently the Dreaditor didn't like *Icicle Bay*, or *Winter Swim*, so every spare bit of paper in the house was gradually filling up with handwritten notes saying *Snowy something-or-other?* and . . . *Cold?*)

Wuffly blinked big brown eyes at Pea, and wagged her tail hopefully.

'I think Wuffly wants to play,' said Pea.

Tinkerbell went on scribbling.

Pea tried rolling the jingly ball under Tinkerbell's chair, but Tinkerbell barely seemed to notice Wuffly's cone-bound head snuffling around her feet. Eventually Pea bounced the ball right into Tinkerbell's lap. With a joyful bark and a supreme effort of tummy-wriggling and balancing on only one back leg, Wuffly managed to perch her hairy grey nose on Tinkerbell's knee. But Tinkerbell pushed her off crossly, snatched up her notebooks, and vanished upstairs without even a glance at the poor dog, shouting, 'I've got homework!' after her.

Wuffly's head sank to the floor and she let out a mournful whine.

'Oh dear, Wuffly's looking droopy again,' said Mum, coming back to refill her tea mug. She ruffled one flopped ear. 'Back to the vee-ee-tee tomorrow, I think.'

But Pea felt certain that this wasn't the sort of droopiness the vee-ee-tee could mend. She knew exactly what was wrong: Wuffly missed Tinkerbell. Pea just didn't know what to do about it. If Pea the pet therapist was going to fix her first patient, she needed some professional advice.

She waited until the sleepy post-apple-pie part of the afternoon, then went next door and rang the bell. Dr Paget and Dr Skidelsky opened the door at once. Dr Skidelsky had her coat on, and was dragging a heavy suitcase. It had shiny gold zips, and wheels on the bottom so you could pull it along.

'Oh – hi, Pea,' she said. 'Here to see Sam, are you? Go on through. Bye, love, I'll text from the station,' she added, giving Dr Paget a kiss. Then she bounced the wheelie case down the driveway, off to catch her train to Scotland.

'Um. Actually,' said Pea, 'it wasn't really Sam I needed to talk to.'

Dr Paget was very understanding. She and Pea sat on the golden sofa in the living room while Pea explained the problem.

'Oh, yes, this is all very familiar,' said Dr Paget. 'Just like family therapy. Very often I'll be brought a case where – for example – an older child has gone back to wetting the bed, like when they were small. It's quite common when something in their life has changed: a new baby in the house, say, or the parents have broken up and Dad's got a new girlfriend. To treat the child's problem, I usually have to treat the people around them too.'

'So,' said Pea, who didn't much want to talk about bed-wetting or broken-up parents when she'd come to ask about a poorly dog, 'to fix Wuffly, you think I need to fix Tinkerbell?'

'Something like that.'

'But that's the whole problem!' said Pea. 'I've told her what she's doing wrong – she doesn't seem to care.'

'I'm sure Tink cares, in her own, er, *special* way,' said Dr Paget. 'But she might not know how to show it, or really understand how what she does affects the dog. So that's what your job will be, as Wuffly's therapist: to find creative ways to involve Tinkerbell in her recovery.'

Pea sighed. Throwing a ball into Wuffly's head-cone was one thing; persuading Tinkerbell to do something she didn't want to was quite another.

Clover was no help.

'I'm doing modelling practice,' she snapped, opening her bedroom door just enough for Pea to see the entire contents of her wardrobe strewn across the carpet, and a peculiar pineapply sort of hair-fountain on top of her head.

Mum was shut in the study, with a Post-it stuck to the door which said:

NO ENTRY
unless you are a magical
book-title fairy who has
invented a new word for
snow

And Klaudia had fallen asleep at the kitchen table halfway through a cup of coffee and a book on paper construction, her broken leg propped up on a chair.

It was still all down to Pea.

That night she lay awake for ages in the dark. It felt odd not to be able to write down her feelings in her diary. Whenever worries swirled around in her head like this, they always seemed clearer once they'd been written down.

A little light suddenly went on in the corner of Pea's mind.

She sat up, turned on the bedside lamp, and hunted through her desk for an empty notebook.

The next morning Pea left the notebook casually lying open in the bathroom, where everyone was sure to see it.

Dear Diary,
My name is Wuffly and I am a dog.

My leg is broken, which makes me sad. Apple pie cheers me up (so long as no one makes rude comments about me getting fat).

I miss running after my best ball, and being able to walk places without hopping.

I miss my owner Tinkerbell, who doesn't play with me any more.

Love from Wuffly

If pointing it out to Tinkerbell herself hadn't worked, maybe hearing it 'direct' from Wuffly would do the trick.

'The diary of a dog,' said Mum at breakfast. 'So clever, Pea! There's a book in that, you know. You'd better hurry up and write it yourself, before I pinch the idea.'

'Mum!' said Clover, sternly wagging her spoon. 'Pea's going to be a pet therapist now, not a writer. Keep up.'

'Anyway, it's not made up, like *your* books,' said Tinkerbell. 'That's what Wuffly *really* thinks.'

'So you did read it, then?' Pea asked.

'Yeah,' said Tinkerbell, through a mouthful of porridge. 'You're *so* clever.'

Then she hopped off her chair and went to get ready for school, without a second glance at poor Wuffly. Pea hoped Mum and Clover might notice – but they were both far too excited about Klaudia's life-drawing class that evening.

After another day at school spent dreading

Mr Ellis's lesson (more underlining: Pea scored 7 out of 25), Pea had lingered behind in the school library, and collected a small pile of books called things like *Know Your Dog* and *Dogs Through History*. She really wanted a quiet evening of research – but since both Mum and Klaudia were going, Pea and Tinkerbell would have to come to Klaudia's class too.

'There'll be loads of art materials and stuff if you want to join in,' Klaudia told them.

'I'll bring my homework project,' said Tinkerbell, clutching a notebook thickly stuffed with paper close to her chest.

'Me too,' said Pea, packing her library books.

One of the strangest things about London was that no matter how long you lived there, there were still entirely new bits to explore. Klaudia's art college was two different buses away; on one of them the Llewellyns all had to stand up so that Klaudia could rest her leg on the only empty seat. Pea had imagined that a college would look quite

113

a lot like a school. Greyhope's was all red brick and windows in little squares – but Klaudia's art college was much too fashionable and London-ish for that. They got off the bus outside an old stone building with pillars, but tucked in between those walls was the entrance to a modern building with huge glass doors.

Klaudia ushered them up a series of slopes, and then through a door marked STUDIO 2. Inside was a cavernous white room, brightly lit. Everywhere you looked was art: half-finished canvases propped up on the floor, covered in blobs of oil paint; a full-sized horse shape made of wire; a coat covered with hundreds of strips of fabric, sewn together in zigzag patterns.

'Works in progress,' said Klaudia airily, stump-ing ahead on her crutches to the far end of the room. 'For the Student Showcase, yeah? We each have to make a piece for this massive exhibition. It's, like, a major deal. I haven't even started yet.'

Beyond these artworks was a circle of easels

already set up, and ten or twelve students standing around chatting – some young and quirky-looking like Klaudia, some old and beardy. Klaudia was immediately surrounded by concerned people, all asking about her leg and fetching her a stool to rest her cast on. Then she shooed them all back to their easels. Mum joined the circle next to her, bobbing her head in little nervous hellos to the other students, as if it were her first day at school. Pea knew just what that felt like, and crossed her fingers secretly for her.

The room fell quiet.

In the centre of the circle was an empty chair. Pea was very glad she was going to be a pet therapist and not a life model. It looked terrifying – like an interrogation room or an execution.

Clover evidently didn't think so.

'Hello, everyone!' she said. 'I'm Clover. I'm your model today – and it's my very first time, so please make me look nice. Thank you!'

As she spoke, she shrugged off her coat to

115

reveal her outfit – a look she had carefully selected from the pile of clothes on her carpet, and termed 'Bohemian Vagabond': velvet shorts from Oxfam, an old baggy white shirt and, from her bag, a bowler hat (borrowed from Tash at school) worn at a jaunty angle. She perched on the edge of the chair in the centre of the circle, one arm raised up over her head, one leg stretched out, and a beaming smile on her face.

'Clover, babe, are you sure you can hold that pose for ten minutes?' said Klaudia, with a frown.

'Yes!' squeaked Clover, without moving her lips.

'OK, then,' said Klaudia. She picked up a tiny golden bell. 'For our new arrivals: we draw for ten minutes, then I ring this dinky little bell – then, Clover, you change position and they draw you again, and so on, for the hour. Ready? Yeah? Go for it!'

She tinkled the little bell, and the artists began to draw. Some used charcoal in big sweeping lines and fingertip smudges. Some, like Mum, had pencils. Some held up bits of cardboard to frame off parts of Clover. Klaudia did a few swift sketches of her own on a drawing board perched on her good knee. Then she walked slowly around the circle, offering little comments: 'Good – good flow,' and 'Don't overwork it,' and 'Clover, keep that arm still, yeah?'

Tinkerbell set to furiously colouring in her mysterious 'homework' using the pastel crayons from the art studio, one crooked arm jealously guarding her handiwork. Pea started to read *Know Your Dog*, but it was hard to concentrate. Her eyes kept flicking between Clover and the clock, counting down the time as her sister's beaming smile began to fade, and her elbow began to droop lower and lower. Ten minutes had never seemed so long.

Apparently Mum didn't think so: from what Pea could see, her picture was nothing more than a few sketchy lines when, at last, Klaudia tinkled the little golden bell.

'Oh, thank you!' breathed Clover, flopping back in the chair. She sprang up and ran over to Mum's easel. 'Let's have a look, then . . .'

But Mum, like all the other artists, was already flipping over to the next blank page.

'Oi, Clover, sit down,' said Klaudia, shooing her. 'Like I told you, remember? Turn the chair so we all get a different angle, yeah? And no hat this time – do something different. Mix it up.'

Clover pouted – the hat had been very carefully selected as part of the ensemble, Pea knew – then spun the hat across the floor, fluffing out her hair where it had been squashed down. She shifted into another pre-planned pose, balancing on one leg and leaning forward slightly, like a runner almost at the finish line. Pea went back to reading Chapter Two: 'How to Have a Happy Puppy' – but every time she glanced up, she was sure Clover was listing further and further to one side as her ankle grew wobblier and wobblier. From the grumbly noises around the circle, everyone else had noticed too.

Clover's next poses were rather less ambitious. When the bell rang for the final time, the students were all drawing Clover slumped in the chair with her elbows propped on her knees and her chin in her hands, looking very bored and cross.

'And that's your lot! Thank you, artists; thank you, model,' said Klaudia.

They all politely clapped. Clover brightened at once, and swept into a bow. Then she hurried out of the circle.

'Oh, wait – no, don't take them!' she said, crestfallen, as the students began to furl up their sketches to take away.

'You don't get to keep the pictures, silly,' said Mum, smiling apologetically at the other students. 'You're only the model.'

One student – an older lady in a red cardigan – took pity on Clover and showed her what she'd drawn. But the paper was covered in individual parts – a nose here, the jut of an elbow there, as if Clover were a shop-window dummy that could be taken apart and not a person at all.

'I don't think I want to be a model after all,' said Clover in a forlorn voice, once the room had emptied. 'I thought they'd be drawing *me*. Not . . . *limbs*.'

'They probably won't want to draw you again, anyway,' said Tinkerbell. 'You did wobble a lot.'

'Shush! You did ever so well for a first try, flower,' said Mum, plonking the bowler hat neatly back on Clover's head.

'So did you, you sly thing,' said Klaudia, punching Mum's arm. 'You've got some real potential there.'

Mum's eyes sparkled as they got her to unfurl her roll of drawings and show them off. They were only vague sketches – no face, just the shape of a body, the tilt of a head – but Pea could see why Klaudia liked them. There was a sort of flow to the lines that seemed natural.

Klaudia's drawings were entirely different: quite scribbly and dark, with lots of jagged lines, and things that hadn't been in the room at all, like giant floating words over Clover's head, or a lion.

'Why is there a lion?' asked Tinkerbell.

'Because of the look on your face right now,' said Klaudia, her usual crazy grin tinged with a faraway look. 'For me, the act of art, it's, like . . . it's not about making a beautiful thing, right?' she explained. 'The world already has beautiful things in it – like you, Clover; like all of you – so it doesn't need artists for that. My art wants to go outwards, like . . . like a mirror you've never looked into before. It's not about the thing I create. It's about the person looking at that thing.'

They were walking out of the studio now, past the wire horse and the unfinished blobby paintings. Pea wondered what a zigzag coat was meant to make the person looking at it feel, apart from warm and like they might be outdoors.

Clover, meanwhile, was looking much reassured by the idea that she was already a beautiful thing. She looked even brighter when one of the students from the class – a youngish man with curly blond hair and a tweedy jacket and glasses – hurried towards them and pressed a small printed card into her hand.

'*Abend, Klaudia! Gefällt mir, dein Bein,*' he said, kissing Klaudia on both cheeks. 'Hi. Sorry. Hi.' He looked like he was thinking of kissing Clover on both cheeks too, then adjusted his glasses and shook her hand instead. 'I'm Willem. I've been coming to Klaudia's class for a while, but I'm a bit of an imposter, really. Not very good at drawing. Photography – that's my thing. I was wondering if you might do some work for me.'

'As a model?' said Clover.

'Yes. I rent a studio – family portraits, mostly, but I do a lot of stock photography for websites, adverts, that sort of thing too. Not high fashion, but . . . you do have the right look. That is, if you don't mind the idea . . .'

'Are you sure she isn't too wobbly?' said Tinkerbell.

'Tink!' said Pea as Clover's face flushed. 'Don't be mean.'

'Oh.' Willem pushed his glasses further up his nose. 'No. That doesn't matter so much with photographs. You just click, and *ping*. Done. If there's any wobbling, I can just take another one.'

'I could definitely stand still long enough to be photographed,' said Clover. 'I think that's much more the sort of modelling that would suit me, actually.'

'Will you pay her?' asked Tinkerbell.

'Tink!' hissed Pea again.

'Um . . .' said Willem, blinking. 'Not much. But yes, a small flat fee for the session.'

Clover bit her lip and looked plaintively at Mum.

Mum was still smiling, off in an artistic dream. 'I don't see why not,' she said distantly. 'If you'd like to. Unless . . .' She shook herself back into Mum mode and had a quick whispered conversation with Klaudia, looking Willem up and down with suitably parental suspicion. Then she smiled again. 'Good. Yes. We'll take your card and I'll give you a call – how's that?'

'Wonderful,' said Willem warmly, and shook Clover's and Klaudia's hands. He looked confused for a moment, then shook Pea's and Tinkerbell's too, since they were there.

'Imagine, me in photographs,' breathed Clover, twirling down the corridor towards the main doors. 'I could be on the side of buses. I could be famous, just for my face. Isn't modelling the very best thing ever?'

Pea thought that being famous just for your face sounded quite horrible – as if it had floated off on its own like all those detached noses and elbows, and the rest of you didn't matter. She'd much rather be famous for *doing* something, like Mum and her books. Or being a pet therapist, obviously. There were probably famous ones of those too.

'Isn't it exciting, us all trying new things?' said Mum.

'We're like a whole new family!' said Clover, spinning around one of Klaudia's crutches.

Tinkerbell hugged her bulging notebook to her chest and grinned rather too enthusiastically.

'I suppose so,' murmured Pea. Being a pet therapist would probably feel more exciting once she was actually any good at it.

When they got home, she spent half an hour fussing over Wuffly – who was not herself at all, and refused even to catch a scrumpled-up paper ball in her head-cone. Tinkerbell, meanwhile, took her 'homework' – whatever it was – upstairs, still tightly clutched in her arms.

Involve her, Dr Paget had said.

But how?

Pea kept on writing Wuffly's diary and 'accidentally' leaving it in places Tinkerbell might see it.

Dear Diary,

I was lonely today because I am a dog and there aren't any other dogs here for me to talk to.

If someone I like would distract me, I expect I might not mind so much.

Love from Wuffly

Dear Diary,

Today we went to the vee-ee-tee. (I know what that means, by the way. I may be a dog but I'm not stupid.)

She took the cone off my head! Hooray! And she says I will be all better in a week or two.

If only there was someone to celebrate it with.

Love from Wuffly

But Tinkerbell kept on missing the point.

'That's dead clever, Pea, reading Wuffly's mind

126

like that,' she would say gleefully. Then out would come the notebook, and she'd spend all evening loitering in the kitchen, one eye monitoring the telephone as if waiting for it to ring.

'What does Tink like *doing* with Wuffly?' asked Sam One when he came round on Friday after school. 'Maybe if you found a way they could do normal-ish things together, that would help?'

Pea nodded. It sounded exactly the right idea. 'But mostly Tink takes her to the park to run around. That's what makes them both happy – only Wuffly still can't do that.'

The vee-ee-tee had said she should start exercising more – but with one leg still in plaster, it wasn't easy.

Klaudia stumped past them on her crutches.

'If only dogs could have those,' said Sam One sadly.

Pea gasped. 'That's it! That's what we need: dog crutches!'

'But, um . . . how?'

'OK, not crutches,' said Pea. 'A wheelchair, maybe. Only dog-sized. And shaped. What about roller skates?'

Wuffly whined.

'OK, not roller skates,' said Pea quickly, petting Wuffly's ears as she pictured the broken leg whizzing off on wheels down a hill while three other hairy legs dragged along behind it. 'We need something more— Oh!'

An image had popped into her head out of nowhere – of walking up to the house next door to ask for help . . .

'When does Dr Skidelsky – I mean, your Mum K – when does she get back from Edinburgh?'

'First thing tomorrow morning,' said Sam One. 'Why?'

Pea beamed. 'Come round the moment she gets home,' she said.

The next day Pea left another diary entry open in the bathroom.

> Dear Diary,
> I would really really really like to go for a run around the park today. Maybe someone might take me?
> Love from Wuffly

Then she waited, knees jigging, in the front room until Sam One knocked at the door. She followed him back to his house and, after a discussion with Dr Skidelsky (who looked tired, and quite un-impressed by the idea of unpacking immediately), Dr Paget fetched a ladder and poked around in the loft. She reappeared with another wheelie case – old and dusty, with no shiny gold zips and a wonky wheel – but the perfect size for a hairy grey dog. Pea wheeled it home at once. It was fiddly arrang-ing the blue blanket and a few cushions inside, to make sure Wuffly's bad leg wouldn't be squashed. But after she'd been gently lifted in, and the old case zipped up so that only her head poked out, she gave a series of little barks that were so joyful and so like her old self that it all seemed instantly worth it.

Even Tinkerbell noticed. At the sound of the barks, she raced downstairs, gave Wuffly's ears a gleeful scruffle, and wrapped Pea in a tight hug.

'She must have asked you to take her for a walk!' she shouted happily, and hurried out of the front door with her scarf and gloves only half on.

Pea, Sam One and Tinkerbell took it in turns to push the suitcase along the bumpy pavements, all the way to the park. Wuffly barked happily at the squirrels. Tinkerbell ran around the duck pond. Pea and Sam One chased after her, pushing the case so Wuffly would feel like she was chasing too. They even let her out to play with the other dogs, and she managed a good three-legged lollop across the grass.

There was a sticky moment on the way home when Tinkerbell ran ahead and turned a corner too fast. The suitcase slipped out of her fingers, picking up speed on the slight downhill slope, and the three of them frantically sprinted after it – but luckily it veered towards a bin, hit it sideways on, and turned over, landing flat on its side. Pea knelt anxiously on the pavement and peered into the case, but Wuffly's eyes were bright, her tongue lolling contentedly out of her mouth and a look of daft dazed contentment on her doggy face.

Once they got home, Pea unzipped the case very carefully. But before she could reach in to lift Wuffly out, she jumped out of her own accord, and went skidding down the hallway. She was still only on three legs, the broken one dragging behind her, but her tail wagged and her head was perkily up. Tinkerbell grabbed the jingly ball, and they hurried off happily together.

'Oh, Pea, you superstar!' whispered Mum, giving her a squeeze. 'Looks like you've fixed them both.'

Pea glowed. Her very first patient was on the mend – and so was the owner.

Dear Diary,
I love my suitcase on wheels!
I would like Tinkerbell to take me for a walk
every single day, please.
Lots of love from Wuffly

CHAPTER 6

KFC

On Saturday afternoon they left Klaudia resting her leg and Clover practising standing on one without wobbling, and went to watch the Kensal Rise Kites play.

On the way out of the house, Pea was almost mown down on the pavement by a string of scruffy muddy girls – Sam Two at the front – in mismatched trackie bottoms and trainers, streaming out of the Paget-Skidelskys. Dr Skidelsky brought up the rear, clutching a red-and-blue football in her arms, a whistle around her neck.

'Come on, Kites, the walk'll warm us up! See you down there, Pea!'

'Go Kites!' yelled Tinkerbell from their own front doorstep, waving her resurrected woollen pompoms. '*Go* Kites!'

Sam Two blushed, and kept her head down as if she hadn't heard, jogging ahead with the others.

Dr Skidelsky hung back. 'I'm sorry, Tinkerbell,' she said. 'Sam's going through a phase where she wants to be with girls more her own age. I hope you don't feel too left out.'

Pea couldn't really blame Sam Two: having a shouty seven-year-old with home-made pompoms around when you were with all your ten-year-old friends was probably quite annoying. She thought Sam Two could be a bit nicer about it, though.

Tinkerbell didn't seem to mind, anyway. She was too busy shoving something white and papery into the front zip pocket of the wheelie case, while Wuffly licked her fingers.

Ten minutes later, Pea and Tinkerbell bounced

Wuffly up over the last kerb and onto the playing fields. They were closely followed by Mum and Dr Paget and Sam One, clutching a huge bundle of bags, towels, water bottles, and what appeared to be collapsible goalposts.

'I can see why the team wants a minibus,' said Mum, her voice muffled behind the cardboard box she was carrying. 'Do you have to cart all this stuff with you for every match?'

Dr Paget nodded. 'If the Kites are playing an away game, the other team have usually got facilities all set up – but when it's at home, it's all down to us.'

They headed for a lumpy field studded with dog poo and with only the faintest hint of white lines marked on the grass.

'Oh,' said Mum as Wuffly whined miserably, bouncing over the bumps in her suitcase. 'This is . . . um . . .'

'Depressing,' sighed Dr Paget.

It really was. Pea's heart sank as she watched

the scruffy team of girls, already fanned out across the grass, collecting up the worst of the dog poo in little plastic bags. Dr Skidelsky rolled them a ball, and they started to kick it between them. Sam Two flicked the ball around quite expertly, tapping it through the other girls' legs or sending it up high – but whenever it hit the ground, it would bounce off in an unexpected sideways direction, or come to a dead halt in an especially soggy dip.

It got worse when the other team arrived. The girls of the Queensbury Royals all had shiny blue shirts and silver-grey socks, and a coach with a logo on the back of her hoodie. The Kites, in their saggy trackie bottoms and grubby trainers, looked sadder than ever.

'It's only clothes,' said Pea, in a sort of hopeful voice. 'I mean, having matching socks doesn't really make you play better, does it?'

'Certainly not,' said Dr Skidelsky, blowing her whistle sharply as she ran onto the pitch.

'But it probably wouldn't hurt,' said Dr Paget,

putting together a very wobbly-looking pair of goalposts.

'Never fear!' announced Tinkerbell, rooting through the zip pocket. She pulled out a squashed roll of paper and unfurled it with a beaming grin. It said:

KFC

in brightly crayoned letters.

'Kentucky Fried Chicken?' said Dr Paget.

'Kites Funraisin Committee!' shouted Tinker-bell, pointing at the words written in smaller handwriting underneath. 'It's my project. I'm going to raise loads and loads of money for the team so when I'm old enough to join, it won't be all sad and pathetic like it is now. You can be my first funraisin people!'

And she dipped into the bag and pulled out an old spaghetti-hoops tin. It had a paper lid with a hole snipped in the top for coins to go through, and *KFC Minibus Fund* crayoned across the side.

'Gosh, you *have* been busy,' said Mum. She poked through her handbag and dropped in 20p.

Dr Paget added a few coppers. 'It's all the change I've got on me – sorry.'

Tinkerbell rattled the tin under Pea and Sam One's noses, but they didn't have any money at all.

By the time Tinkerbell had thrust the tin at everyone on the field (most of whom were players, though she spent a long time talking to a round-faced, black-haired lady on the touchline), she'd made £1.28 and a chocolate button.

'I thought there'd be more spectators,' she said, frowning.

'Minibuses are expensive, Tinky-wink,' said Mum. 'It might be better to aim a bit lower.'

But Tinkerbell shrugged this off. 'Oh, don't worry. The KFC has got tons of other funraisin plans.'

Mum looked alarmed, but before she could ask,

there was a sharp whistle from Dr Skidelsky and the match began.

Pea had never been especially interested in football, but Tinkerbell's dad Clem was a massive fan. Years ago, they had spent summer Saturdays on the sofa, cheering on his beloved Birmingham City while Mum locked herself in the kitchen to write the very first *Mermaid Girls* book. This match was a little different from the ones she'd seen before – the teams were seven-a-side, and they swapped players on and off the pitch more often to give them a rest – but even Pea could see two things right away: first, that Sam Two was the best player on the pitch by far; and second, that it wasn't going to make any difference. The Queensbury Royals had proper football boots with studs in the soles, so they didn't skid around in the mud like all the Kites. They had to cope with the uneven ground, which made the ball bounce up oddly – but they kicked at the goal as if they expected success. The Kites, even Sam Two, kicked as if they expected the goalposts to fall over (which they did, twice, before half-time).

Dr Skidelsky tried lots of different tactics, Pea could see: swapping players around, giving people longer rests. Tinkerbell gave her all on the touch-line, shouting and waving her raggedy pompoms as if volume alone might make the ball bounce through the posts. But it was not enough. When the final whistle blew, the score was Royals: 11, Kites: nil.

'Well done, girls, that was loads better than last week!' shouted Dr Skidelsky.

Sam Two glared at her as one of the wobbly goalposts fell over again.

Pea bit her lip as the Queensbury Royals giggled, and climbed into their minibus. It was just so unfair.

When they got home, at least there was good news. Clover pressed the phone excitedly into Mum's hand.

'Willem called,' she said. 'The photographer

from the art class? He's got a spare session at his studio and he wants me to come and do modelling. Call him back? Please? Now?'

Mum had to call Willem back while Clover stood frozen beside her like a perfect wobble-free statue, hands on her lips, listening to his mumbly hesitant voice on the phone.

'Next weekend, mhmm,' said Mum, writing down an address.

Clover's eyes went enormously wide.

'How much is he going to pay?' asked Tink, jingling the KFC tin. 'Supermodels make thousands. We could buy a whole minibus by next week!'

'*Eugh*, go away – that tin still smells like spaghetti hoops,' said Clover. 'And why has it got *Kentucky Fried Chicken* written on the side?'

Tinkerbell started to explain about the KFC and the 'funraisin', till Mum told them both to shush.

'Well?' said Clover, once Mum had hung up.

'He'll take some pictures next Saturday. I'll come

141

with you, to make sure it's all sensible, and sign a release form. And no, he's not going to give you thousands, but he will pay you a small fee. Which will be Clover's money, not the KFC's – though if she decided to donate some of it to the Kites, I think that would be a lovely, generous thing to do.'

Mum tucked Clover's hair behind her ear, and gave her a little questioning look. 'Are you sure this is what you want to do?'

'Yes. And I'll *definitely* think about making a small donation,' said Clover.

'I wish I could help too,' said Pea. In the old days she'd have offered to write a story, or perhaps a play for Clover's Drama Club to perform – but it was hard to see how a budding pet therapist could raise money for matching socks.

'Don't worry, you will,' said Tinkerbell, giving Pea a wide and worrying grin.

On Sunday morning, before anyone had dressed or eaten breakfast, the doorbell rang. Tinkerbell zoomed downstairs to answer. By the time Pea and Mum arrived, a round-faced, black-haired woman was climbing back into her car and driving off, while a small, faintly familiar girl waved from the back seat.

On the chilly doorstep was a wooden crate containing two rabbits; a cardboard box with a tortoise inside; and a bowl with a goldfish in it. Wedged beneath the goldfish was an envelope with money poking out, and a handmade advert, coloured in, in Tinkerbell's handwriting.

PEA LLEWELLYN: DOG WHISPERER
Poorly pups, limp Labradors, tantrumming
terriers?
Pea can make them happy again!
All other small pets considered

Please call 020 798343 and ask for
Tinkerbell to make an appointment
£10 per consultation — all funds to go to
the KFC

143

'Oh,' said Pea.

'Oh *no*,' said Mum.

'Oh *hooray*!' said Tinkerbell, holding up a fistful of notes. 'Thirty pounds for the KFC!'

CHAPTER 7

WORK, WORK, WORK

'It's for a good cause!' protested Tinkerbell.

'I can see that, my piglet,' said Mum, looking at the small zoo now sitting on the doorstep. 'But you can't just turn the house into an animal hospital without any warning! Did you even ask Pea if she wanted to help?'

Tinkerbell frowned. 'No. But I thought she might say no if I did. No one ever really wants to do funraisin things: they're always horrible torture-ish stuff like Sponsored Sitting in a Bath of Beans. Anyway, I had to wait to see if she fixed Wuffly, or we might have to give refunds. It's all right, though. She really *can* read animals' minds – so I know she can mend these ones.'

Pea felt her stomach go knotty. It was nice, having a little sister who believed in her magical mind-reading powers so completely – but it wasn't true.

'But where did they come from?' said Mum.

'It was Mrs Bianco in the car,' said Tinkerbell, as if anyone else had any clue who Mrs Bianco might be. 'Duh, Mum. Her daughter Sallyanne is one of the Kites. Blinky belongs to her.'

She picked the tortoise up out of the cardboard box. The word BLINKY was written across its back in turquoise nail polish.

'What's wrong with it?' asked Pea warily. It didn't look like a proper tortoise at all. Its arms and legs and head were all tucked possessively away into its shell – though she could see a rubbery-looking tail poking out of its bottom like a poo.

'Some kind of sleeping sickness, Sallyanne says,' Tinkerbell explained. 'It was fine and walking around last week, and now it's gone all quiet. And it's not eating anything, either. The goldfish is called Bubbles. That belongs to Sallyanne's big brother.'

'Well, we can see what's wrong there,' said Mum, peering into the bowl.

Bubbles was swimming around like any other goldfish, but its body had a definite lean to one side, as if gravity wasn't quite working under the water.

'And the rabbits?' asked Pea, peering anxiously in through the gaps in the wooden crate's slats. There seemed to be a lot of jumping and wriggling about going on in there, and she kept her fingers well out of the way.

'Tulip and Rosie,' said Tinkerbell as Pea gingerly pried open the lid just enough for them to peep in. 'They belong to Mrs Bianco's next-door neighbours. They've had Tulip for years and years, she said, and they got Rosie to keep her company, but they keep fighting.'

Tinkerbell was not wrong. All they could see

through the gap in the lid was a blur of white floppy ears and teeth, accompanied by snapping noises.

Putting the lid down very firmly, Pea – still in her pyjamas – carried the crate out into the garden at once. There was still early February frost on the patio that made the bottoms of her slippers wet, so she put the crate up on the patio table, and fetched towels to drape over the top to keep the rabbits warm. But then Rosie bit Tulip, and Tulip bit Rosie back, and they fought so hard they turned the crate over and spilled themselves out into the garden. They hopped about, sniffing the wet grass, leaping away the moment Pea tried to get close. Wuffly emerged to chase after them ineffectually on three legs, barking madly until both rabbits scurried back into the upturned crate, their noses twitching in fear. Then they started fighting again.

'Get me another box!' yelped Pea, slamming the lid back on the crate and sitting on it, shivering, while the rabbits fought.

Tinkerbell darted inside. A few minutes later she returned with a blue plastic storage box from her bedroom that usually held lots of Lego.

'I thought we could use this for a lid so it can breathe,' she said, holding up a wire rack from the oven.

'It'll have to do for now,' said Pea, taking a deep breath before rolling up her pyjama sleeve and plunging her hand into the crate. She plucked out a wriggly Tulip (at least, she guessed it might be Tulip – it was the big white one, anyway) and, with difficulty, wedged her flailing legs into the blue box. The wire rack wouldn't stay on by itself, so she added hinges made from parcel tape. She put it next to Rosie's crate, and made sure both rabbits were very securely sealed in.

Then she went inside and hugged a radiator to warm up.

Finding temporary homes for the goldfish and the tortoise was much easier. Once she was dressed, Pea put BLINKY back in her cardboard box (she was guessing about the 'her', but BLINKY seemed like it might be a girl's name), and set it on the desk in her attic bedroom until she could do a bit more research on how to talk to reptiles – specifically ones that wouldn't wake up.

Bubbles the goldfish went in Mum's study, on the book shelf. Mum wasn't especially happy about having a study guest, but Pea promised that Bubbles would provide very helpful inspiration for writing about mermaids, especially imperfect ones that were poorly.

Then she went inside and wrote a list at the kitchen table, while Mum and Tinkerbell made toast and tea for breakfast.

SHOPPING:
Lettuce (check that rabbits like lettuce)
Goldfish food
Tortoise food (might be lettuce again?)
Big book about rabbits/goldfish/tortoises

'*Morgen*,' mumbled Klaudia, wobbling out of her little bedroom on her crutches. '*Ach!* Morning, I mean, morning. Sorry, was just chatting to my vati on the phone – my brain's still in German.' She grabbed her ear, twisting it and making a *click* noise, as if she really did have a switch in her head to flip between the two.

'Sorry if we woke you up,' said Tinkerbell.

Pea winced as the sound of an angry rabbit flinging itself against the bars of an oven rack echoed in from the garden. Klaudia looked very sleepy. She was still wearing her clothes from yesterday, and her faded purple hair stood on end.

'No, no, I haven't really been to sleep, actually,' said Klaudia, making herself a cup of coffee with hot water from the tap, and gulping it down.

Pea nodded sympathetically. Mum sometimes stayed up all night writing, when there was a particularly exciting mermaidy thing happening in her chapter. Not that she'd been doing that much lately; she was more likely to stay up talking to

151

Klaudia about art. The random notes of possible book titles (*Frosty Midnight? Frozen Twilight? Chilly Wednesday?*) were now covered in sketchy doodles of pirates, and moonlit shipwrecks. Mum had even started to dress more like Klaudia. Today she was wearing dangly turquoise earrings, and three different loopy scarves around her neck.

Pea thought back to what Mum had said about wanting to be an artist, and what Klaudia had said about her own art, at the college – how it was meant to be like a mirror you'd never looked into before. Did Mum still see a writer when she looked in the mirror? Pea had been staring into the one in the bathroom a lot lately, to check if a pet therapist looked back, but mostly she just saw a freckly girl with a big chin.

'Have you started on your self-portrait for the Student Showcase?' asked Pea, noticing the pencil stuck behind Klaudia's ear and trying to peep through the not-quite-closed bedroom door. After seeing Klaudia's strange pictures of Clover with a lion, and her tin of *Klaudia* paint, she was itching to see what a Klaudia self-portrait might look like.

'Don't be nosy, Pea-nut,' said Mum. 'You know how much I hate showing people my work before it's finished.'

'Not much to look at yet anyway – soz.' Klaudia tapped the side of her forehead. 'The magic is all up here still. At least, I hope it is . . .'

With a deep frown, she picked up her crutches and headed back into her room, closing the door firmly behind her.

Mum, Tinkerbell and Pea took Wuffly out in the wheelie case for a three-legged run around Queen's Park. On the way home they bought lettuces, carrots and bedding for the rabbits, then they picked up a tub of goldfish food and some special swim-bladder medicine from Mrs Dean at the pet shop. She didn't have a big book about rabbits and goldfish and tortoises, but she gave Pea some leaflets instead.

'That medicine had better fix whatever's wrong

with Bubbles,' said Tinkerbell sadly, counting out their change as they left the shop. 'That's probably half a minibus steering wheel in that tiny weeny bottle.'

Pea hoped it would work too, and not only for the sake of the KFC.

Every day that week, she got up early to chop lettuce and carrots, to drip medicine into Bubbles's bowl, and to check BLINKY's box.

Every evening after school, she'd sit in the garden with the crate and the blue plastic box, reading her leaflets. It was very chilly, even wearing a woolly hat, so she added lots of extra bedding for the rabbits, and a plastic sheet from next door over the top to keep out draughts and raindrops.

Not that the rabbits seemed to appreciate it. Pea had always wanted a rabbit when she was Tink's age. She would've called it Thumper. But they'd been living on a houseboat in Norway at the time, and after that a basement flat where they all shared one room and there wasn't any garden, or spare money for rabbit food. She hadn't imagined rabbits like Tulip and Rosie, anyway; her imaginary Thumper was all quivery-nosed and gentle, and sat sweetly in her arms while she stroked its ears. The reality (Tulip lunging at the oven-rack bars, Rosie snapping at her fingers) was quite disappointing.

She peered into their eyes a lot, and said soothing things, but it wasn't at all like it was with Wuffly. She had no idea at all why they were so grumpy.

The wonky goldfish was a mystery too.

And though she tried at first, there seemed no sense at all in saying soothing things to a cardboard box full of uneaten lettuce and a tortoise that still showed no sign of owning a head or any legs.

Pea felt quite out of her depth.

'Are all the animals nearly fixed yet?' asked Tinkerbell, over breakfast on Saturday morning. 'Only I think Mrs Bianco said she'd phone today for an update.'

Panicking, Pea put a huge spoonful of cornflakes in her mouth to give her time to think of an answer. To her relief, before she'd finished chewing Clover came twirling into the kitchen, looking *very* distracting in a slithery white camisole, striped tights and a red tutu.

'What do you think?' she said, spinning in a circle before plonking the familiar bowler hat jauntily on her head. 'It's for my photoshoot with Willem. Tash from school lent me the tutu. Ballerinas are very *now*, apparently.'

'Um,' said Mum. 'It looks a bit . . . cold.'

'She means tarty,' said Tinkerbell, licking jam off her toast.

Clover's eyes went very wide.

'I do not!' exclaimed Mum hotly. 'I'd never say that. Only, well – you might want to cover up just a tiny bit more, darling. How about the big woolly jumper you got me for Christmas?'

'Mu-um!' said Clover, folding her arms crossly. 'That's stripy. I can't have a stripy top *and* stripy legs; that's not sophisticated and model-like at all.'

'You could wear the jumper with something

else on the bottom, then, flower. Like, trousers, maybe?'

Clover stuck out her chin and stomped upstairs, muttering about philistines and being tragically misunderstood. The sound of sniffing wafted down the stairs. Tinkerbell and Pea went to investigate. Clover was lying face down on her bed, clutching a box of tissues to her chest.

'It's very hard trying to be a model,' she sobbed into her pillow, 'especially when people say you're too wobbly or don't understand about stripes. I helped you both with *your* new future careers!'

'You said my KFC tin smelled like spaghetti hoops!' said Tinkerbell.

'Well, it does – you should've washed it properly. Anyway, I said I'd give you some of my model money. You should want me to be a famous brilliant model!'

Tinkerbell looked hopefully at Pea.

'What can we do to help?' asked Pea.

Clover perked up immediately, and began

emptying her wardrobe onto the rumpled bed. 'Help me find the perfect outfit for my very first photoshoot?'

The next half-hour was spent on a miniature fashion show for Mum, and Klaudia too once she'd been coaxed out of bed with hot coffee. Tinkerbell was in charge of hair bobbles and shoes. Pea did up zips and came up with each look's special name: 'Downtown Vintage', 'Mumsy Sparkle' and – her personal favourite – 'Crazy Cardigans', which involved wearing three at once, in layers. Mum and Klaudia made suitable 'Gosh, wow, lovely' noises whenever Clover looked especially anxious.

In the end, it was Klaudia who saved the day, suggesting that the denim shorts from 'Downtown Vintage' would look great with the original tutu and tights, and a plain black top.

'Quirky on the bottom, simple on the top,' she said. 'You'd fit in at my college no problem.'

It was the perfect thing to say. Mum and Clover dashed off to their appointment with Willem

158

together, Clover now only slightly red around the eyes.

'We'll be back for lunch!' Mum called over her shoulder.

Klaudia, Pea and Tinkerbell took Wuffly to the vee-ee-tee, who snipped off Wuffly's plaster cast with a big pair of scissors. Then they went for her first wheelie-case-less walk around the park. Wuffly couldn't run quite as fast as usual, but she barely even limped, much to Klaudia's disgust. *She'd* been back to the hospital the day before, and her cast would be staying where it was for another few weeks; maybe even longer.

'At least a broken leg doesn't stop you making art,' said Tinkerbell helpfully.

'Hmm.' Klaudia didn't sound convinced.

Back at home, Klaudia disappeared into her room to work. Very loud German rock music – the kind where the singing is mostly shouting – began to reverberate from behind her door, echoing through the whole house.

'It helps me think! Inspiration!' Klaudia yelled over the noise, when Pea went to ask if she was feeling all right.

Pea had no idea how that sort of noise could help anyone think. The singer sounded cross, but from what she could remember from living in the commune, most things did when you said them in German.

Pea escaped to the study. She turned on Mum's computer, put her fingers in her ears, and read everything she could from *SmallAnimalCare.com* while Bubbles splished encouragingly on the book shelf. By the time Mum and Clover came home, Klaudia's music had gone quiet, and Pea had made one very important discovery.

'BLINKY's *meant* to be asleep! Tortoises hibernate in winter. If she was awake and wandering around last week, it's only because someone must have put her somewhere warm by mistake – which made her think it was time to wake up. But really she needs to be left in her box somewhere cool.

She doesn't even need lettuce or anything.'

'Well done, you clever thing,' said Mum, stroking Pea's frizzy ponytail.

'You can even read *sleeping* minds,' said Tinkerbell proudly.

Mum gave Pea a look, as if waiting for her to put Tinkerbell right – but Clover couldn't hold in her news any longer.

'Modelling's amazing!' she said breathlessly. 'Willem says I have the perfect look for adverts in magazines, and he's sure someone will buy my pictures. He's got this lovely studio space, so light and airy. And he doesn't have a little bell that rings between poses, or worry about wobbling. I just had to smile a bit, and point, and laugh even though there wasn't anything funny, and then he gave Mum a cheque, all for me. Isn't it amazing?'

'I suppose,' said Pea, though Mum looked more worried than thrilled.

'So you'll be in adverts for things you don't know about?' asked Tinkerbell. 'Like, pointing and smiling at a pizza that you haven't eaten? But that's lies!'

Clover fluffed her blonde waves around her ears. 'You're so naive, Tink, darling. Adverts aren't true. It's all airbrushing and computer-generated eyebrow hairs these days. Not that they'll have to do any of that with *my* picture. Will they, Mum?' she said, suddenly anxious.

'If someone buys your picture from Willem, I suppose they could do anything they liked to it. Which is why we're just trying this out – right, flower? And never forgetting that you are wonderful for reasons that are much more important than what you look like. Yes?'

'Don't worry,' said Clover. 'I'm not going to let anyone start taking pictures of me in my bra or anything. My impending huge fame won't go to my head at all. And of course I'll be donating some of my fee to the KFC,' she added grandly.

Tinkerbell grinned.

'At least some of us are having a good day,' said Klaudia, sighing as she emerged from her room, looking rumply and tired again.

'Oh dear. How's the self-portrait?' asked Mum.

'It isn't,' replied Klaudia. 'Not one idea in my head. I'm starting to think maybe when you break your leg, all your inspiration might, like, drip out of you through the crack in your bones.'

'Urgh. Really?' Tinkerbell looked sideways at Wuffly.

'No, not really,' said Mum.

But as the day went on into evening, and Klaudia's 'inspirational' work music got louder and louder, Pea did start to wonder.

Mum tried working in the study wearing Pea's earmuffs, but in the end she took her bundle of notebooks off to the café down the road. Clover tried to block it out with singing. Eventually, after a polite phone call from the Paget-Skidelskys at around six p.m., Clover, Pea and Tinkerbell pushed open Klaudia's bedroom door to turn it off. They found her lying fast asleep on the floor, her leg stretched out and a pencil in each hand, surrounded by screwed-up sheets of paper.

Tinkerbell clicked the music off, and they all reeled for a moment in the sudden silence.

Klaudia didn't stir.

'Artist's block,' Clover sighed, pulling a blanket over her. They'd all seen Mum in a similar state – at her desk for days in front of a blank screen and a mockingly winky cursor.

'She did say all her inspiration had fallen out through the crack in her bones,' whispered Pea.

They looked at one another, stricken with guilt. If that was true, it was *their* fault, sort of; if Wuffly had never run out into the road . . .

'Maybe we can help?' whispered Tinkerbell. 'Sam One's good at drawing. We could get him to do some of it for her. No one would need to know.'

Clover shook her head. 'That would be cheating. Like getting someone else to do your home-work for you.'

'OK. Then we'll just have to be really, really inspiring from now on.'

Pea nodded, thinking hard.

Klaudia made an extra-loud snorty snore, so they hurried out of the bedroom, gently closing the door behind them. Then Pea went to Mum's study and found some fresh Post-it notes.

Dear Mum of Pea,
I am going to stay with Klaudia for a little while, because she needs artistic inspiration, and you are already really good at writing books about fish women. Please try not to mind too much.
Love from Bubbles

Dear Klaudia,

My name is Bubbles. I thought perhaps you would like to draw me? It might help you feel more inspired for your self-portrait. (I am not really meant to be swimming sort of sideways, so if you could draw me a bit more normal-looking, that would be politest.)

Love from Bubbles

Pea left the second note sticky-taped to the goldfish bowl on the kitchen table, so that Klaudia wouldn't knock it over with her leg when she woke up.

On Sunday it was the Paget-Skidelskys' turn to cook lunch. Sam Two played her football game on the console while Tinkerbell watched. Sam One worked on his new comic, *Space Ant vs. the Elephants of Mars.* Pea longed to join in and help (there were spelling mistakes, and no elephants yet even though he was on page six) – but she held firm, and took Wuffly for a therapeutic run around the garden instead.

There wasn't any apple pie this time, but Mum and Clover had made banana cake instead. Wuffly gave it a sniff, but turned her nose up at it. (Pea didn't blame her: banana cake wasn't anywhere near as good as apple pie.)

Clover told them all about her photograph session with Willem.

'And I hear you're becoming quite the pet-therapy superstar,' said Dr Skidelsky to Pea.

Pea shuffled her shoulders, embarrassed. 'It's definitely easier with dogs. The goldfish just goes round and round, so it's a bit hard to tell if it's happy or not. And the rabbits are still fighting.'

'Two rabbits?' said Dr Paget, pouring out cups of coffee.

'Yes,' said Pea. 'It's understandable, I think,

167

because Tulip used to live on her own, and Rosie's new – and quite bitey – so I think Tulip doesn't like having to share. I've put them in different houses next to each other so they can make friends without any more fighting, but I'm not sure it's working. Rosie still keeps trying to get into Tulip's house.'

Dr Paget smiled. 'I see. I used to have rabbits when I was small. The females can be awfully moody.'

Pea shook her head, happy to have hit on one thing she was sure about. 'Actually, Tulip is a boy rabbit; Rosie's the girl. I've got a book that shows you the differences,' she added quietly, not sure if it was the sort of thing you were supposed to talk about at Sunday lunch.

'Hmm,' said Dr Paget, eyes sparkling as she looked at Mum and Dr Skidelsky.

'Ahh,' said Dr Skidelsky.

'Oh dear,' said Mum weakly. 'Pea-pod, I don't think they're fighting. I think they're trying to make babies.'

Pea felt her face flush very, very pink. Making babies was *definitely* not the sort of thing you were supposed to talk about at Sunday lunch. But the Paget-Skidelskys didn't seem shocked at all, and explained it to Tinkerbell quite comfortably, without any giggling. It made Pea feel extremely grown up.

'So will there be lots of baby rabbits soon, then?' asked Sam One.

Tinkerbell's face lit up – but Dr Skidelsky shook her head.

'Hopefully not, if Pea separated them quickly enough.'

'That's a good thing, Tink, honestly,' said Mum. 'Rabbits can have loads of babies, not just one. Ten extra mouths to feed? That's a lot of lettuce and carrots.'

Tinkerbell frowned. Pea could almost see her counting what was left of the KFC fund in her head.

'We could sell them, for funraisin,' said Tinkerbell, eating the end of the banana cake.

'They aren't even our rabbits!' exclaimed Mum. 'And with any luck, there won't be any more! But we should get that properly checked, I think. We'll take Rosie to the vet this week, Pea.'

At the sound of the v-word, Wuffly bolted, and attempted to leap over Sam Two. Dr Skidelsky (who was not at all a dog person) knocked over her coffee cup as she flung her arms up in panic, scooting her chair backwards. Wuffly landed in a whiny heap of legs and podgy tummy on Pea's lap, licked her face, then slithered onto the floor and bounded away, dragging her unbandaged but still rather droopy leg behind her.

'Vee-ee-tee! I meant vee-ee-tee!' shouted Mum. Once they'd mopped up the coffee and Pea had soothed poor Wuffly, Mum decided it was time to go.

'Little rabbit babies . . .' sighed Clover dreamily as they walked back into their own house.

'Let's hope not, eh?' said Mum.

'We don't need the vee-ee-tee, Mum,' said

Tinkerbell crossly. 'Just get Pea to check. She can read Rosie's mind and find out.'

'Duh, Tink,' said Clover, strolling ahead. 'Pea can't *really* read animals' minds!'

Pea froze in the hallway.

Tinkerbell gazed up at her. 'Is that true?' she whispered.

Pea bit her lip, and nodded guiltily.

Tinkerbell frowned, then shrugged her shoulders. 'OK.'

Pea blinked. 'You aren't cross?'

Tinkerbell shrugged again. 'Not really. I mean, if you think about it, it was a bit unlikely, wasn't it?'

Pea allowed herself a little smile of relief – but before she could relax, there was a wail from the kitchen.

'Pea, oh, Pea!' yelped Clover, her voice high and frightened.

Pea ran down the hall at once, because Clover could be silly and far too dramatic, but her voice

171

only ever quavered that way when something really, truly awful had happened.

At the kitchen door, Pea stopped still and put her hands to her lips.

The goldfish bowl was on the kitchen table, still with her handwritten note attached. On the surface of the water floated Bubbles, quite dead.

CHAPTER 8

A GOODBYE

Pea went upstairs to her attic bedroom, lay down, and cried until her face hurt. Clover brought her a toilet roll when she ran out of tissues from the box. Then she cried some more.

Downstairs, she could hear Mum's voice on the phone to Mrs Bianco, explaining about BLINKY and the rabbits, working very slowly up to the bad news.

'We are so, so sorry,' she said calmly. 'Of course, we'll bring . . . um . . . we'll bring the bowl and the, um, body back to . . . Oh. Oh, well, if you think . . . Of course, I see, yes . . . Yes. So sorry.'

Then Mum came upstairs and sat on Pea's bed. 'They said,' she told her in a soft voice, 'that no one really bothered much about the goldfish, and that ... and that ... and that we should flush Bubbles down the toilet.'

It was too awful. Pea buried her face in Mum's neck.

'Poor Bubbles! Imagine if someone said that about Wuffly!' wailed Clover, who had been hovering with more toilet rolls at the bottom of the attic stairs. She thudded up them at once to join in. Tinkerbell crept up after her, Wuffly clutched awkwardly in her arms, and all five of them made a sad, soggy knot on Pea's bed, curled up together.

'It's all my fault,' croaked Pea eventually. 'I wanted to practise being a pet therapist some more, like with Wuffly. But Bubbles should've gone to a proper vee-ee-tee, not me.'

'Oh, Pea-pod,' said Mum, smoothing her hair. 'I don't think a real vee-ee-tee could've helped a goldfish.'

'Mrs Dean in the pet shop did say they were tricky to look after,' said Tinkerbell.

'Did she?' asked Clover.

Pea sniffed, and nodded.

'Well, that explains it,' said Clover. 'You bought that medicine. You were trying, after all. I think sometimes things just die, don't they, Mum? And it isn't anyone's fault. It just happens.'

Pea squeezed Clover's hand gratefully, and they all blew their noses.

'We aren't really going to flush it down the toilet, are we?' asked Tinkerbell.

'Certainly not,' said Mum. 'We'll give Bubbles a proper send-off. What do you think, my starlets? What should a goldfish funeral look like?'

Pea thought hard. It ought to be something watery, really. Perhaps they could go to the Thames and send it off in a boat on fire, like a Viking. But that would mean finding a boat (a very small, gold-fish-sized one) – and then what if the fire went out after they'd launched it? Or set fire to something

175

else? No, something more simple would be best.

'I think we should bury Bubbles in the garden,' she said, 'so we can leave flowers and things, and we won't ever forget. If no one minds having a grave just outside the house, I mean.'

No one minded; they all thought it was just right.

'You should think of something to say, Pea,' said Clover, 'since you knew Bubbles the best. Like a poem, maybe? And there should definitely be singing. I can do that.'

'It's not an audition, you weirdo,' said Tinkerbell.

'Tink!' said Mum. 'Clover's right – funerals usually have music. Something sad, or something the deceased really liked to listen to.'

Pea didn't know what songs Bubbles liked to listen to. The only music she was certain Bubbles had ever heard was Klaudia's German shouting, and no one could possibly want that at their funeral. In the end Clover settled on 'For Those in Peril on the Sea'.

Mum went next door to invite the Paget-Skidelskys round for a brief service in the back garden at six p.m.

Tinkerbell put herself in charge of gravestone construction, and disappeared into Klaudia's room. Then they went off together to the shops, though they wouldn't say why.

Pea lay on her bed, trying to think what she could say at a funeral for a fish that she really – to be honest – had never known all that well, and had only ever seen in a wonky state of ill-health. Just before six, she changed into her darkest blue jeans and a black jumper, and went solemnly downstairs. Mum was in the kitchen, sniffling over a small flattish parcel made from kitchen towels.

'Is that . . . ?' Pea asked.

Mum nodded. 'I thought we should put it in something, and, well, leftover Christmas wrapping paper didn't seem quite right. Do you want to . . . ?' She picked up the parcel and offered it to Pea.

Pea recoiled at once, and Mum nodded and

took the parcel outside, so no one had to look at it any longer than they needed to. Through the back door, Pea could see Dr Paget, the two Sams and Klaudia, already waiting.

Clover and Tinkerbell arrived on either side of Pea, both also dressed in nearly-black. (Tinkerbell had her glow-in-the-dark skeleton pyjama top on, which wasn't the ideal thing to wear to a funeral, but she had at least turned it inside out so you almost couldn't tell.) Pea felt both her hands being held tightly, then all three sisters stepped out into the gloomy early evening.

There was already a small hole dug in the flower-bed closest to the wall between the two houses.

'I made the hole. Is it in the right sort of place?' asked Sam One nervously.

Pea nodded. It was perfect: next to a tree, so it would be shady in summer.

'Kara had to go back to Edinburgh, Pea – sorry,' said Dr Paget. 'But she sends her love and sympathy for your loss.'

Pea nodded again. Clover, on her left, squeezed her hand even tighter.

'So,' said Mum. 'Er . . . I hereby lay Bubbles to rest.'

She knelt down and gently placed the parcel in the hole. There was a green plastic spade – the kind you take to the beach – lying on the grass. Mum offered it to Pea, but she shook her head, so Mum scooped up a few spadefuls of earth and filled in the hole.

Pea mostly looked at the darkening sky as she did it, blinking a lot.

'I didn't have much time,' said Klaudia, clearing her throat, 'so it's not all completely dry yet – but I thought this might be better than, like, an ordinary sort of headstone.' She was still balancing on her crutches, so she nodded to Sam One, who ducked down behind her.

It was Bubbles's goldfish bowl, now painted all over with glossy transparent paint in blues and greens and golds.

Dr Paget pushed a small white candle into the earth, then lit it. Very carefully, Sam One lowered the glass goldfish bowl over the flame, upside-down. He tucked a stone under the lip, so that enough air could get in to keep the candle burning. Then he stood back so they could all see.

The flame glowed from inside the bowl, lighting up the colours like stained glass. The flickering of the candle made it seem as if the painted water was moving.

'Oh, how lovely,' said Dr Paget.

'Beautiful,' agreed Mum. 'Thank you, Klaudia.'

Pea looked at Klaudia too, and nodded a lot, not trusting herself to speak.

'Did you want to say something, darling?' asked Mum.

Pea fumbled in her pocket and produced a torn-out page from her notebook. It had been so difficult to know what to write, now that she wasn't a writer any more.

Goodbye Bubbles
by Pea Llewellyn

Farewell Bubblefish
We are sad that you have died
Swim straight in heaven.

'It's a haiku,' she explained, stuffing it back in her pocket. 'That's why it's so short – not because I didn't like Bubbles or anything like that.'

Mum nodded very understandingly. Then Clover stepped forward and sang her song. Tinkerbell reached into a plastic bag at her feet and pulled out a little plastic pot of bubble mixture. As Clover sang, she blew long streams of bubbles. Most popped at once, but a few sturdy ones rose into the sky, drifting over the high wall and off into the night. It made everyone smile, even Sam Two.

They smiled even more when Wuffly lunged

out of the back door and began bounding unsteadily around the garden, snapping at the bubbles. Every now and then one would land on her nose, and she would look utterly dismayed and sit down – only to leap up again the moment she saw another.

Pea found herself laughing, and felt terrible – for who laughs at a funeral? – but Mum said that Bubbles would be so pleased that its name had become a way to make them all happy again, and she thought laughing was probably allowed, after all. With one last sad look at the little patch of earth and the glowing candle, Pea gave Bubbles a small wave goodbye, and they all went inside.

Sam One stayed to watch a DVD with Pea – but it was one where a fish died, so they stopped partway through and played Monopoly instead.

'Mum Gen says it's the hardest thing about being a therapist,' Sam One told Pea. 'Having a patient who you can't help.'

'I did try,' she said.

'Oh yeah. You tried loads,' said Sam One, nodding a lot.

'Only it still wasn't enough,' Pea sighed. 'Being a pet therapist isn't at all like I expected, Sam. I thought there'd be fluffy little things to look after, and I could mend them with a plaster or by cheering them up. But you have to clean out boxes that smell like wee, and not mind getting your fingers bitten. And when it goes wrong, it's just *awful*.'

'So stop doing it, then,' said Sam One, tapping his top hat across the board to Fleet Street.

Pea was so startled she forgot to ask him for his £18 rent. (Sam One paid it anyway.) It had never crossed her mind that she could just stop – but he was right. It was the only thing to do. After they finished the game and packed it away, they went to find Mum to tell her to call Mrs Bianco back and get her to come and collect BLINKY, Tulip and Rosie as soon as possible.

Pea whispered a near-silent farewell through the air holes of BLINKY's cardboard box, and left it on the bottom of the stairs. She and Sam One fed two last sad carrots to the rabbits.

Then she went to the fridge, carefully crossed out *pet therapist* on her CV, and added another '?'.

PEA
Age: 11
Current occupation: schoolgirl
Likes: books
Special skills: writing, reading,
  making sandwiches
Future career: ~~writer (like Mum)~~ ?
          ~~pet therapist~~ ?

'What will you be now?' asked Sam One.

Pea shook her head anxiously. 'I just don't know.'

That night, Pea brushed her teeth and got ready for bed as usual, then crept down the corridor to Clover's room. It was at the back of the house, overlooking the garden, and from the window she could look down and see the goldfish bowl. To her relief, the candle under the glass was still glowing very faintly in the darkness – but as she watched, it flickered once, twice, then grew dimmer and dimmer until it was gone. Her eyes filled with fresh tears. It was all so overwhelming: the funeral, and being a scary question mark again . . .

Now that she was at the back of the house, she could hear Klaudia's music throbbing up through the floorboards. It was the same old horrible shouty kind, much too loud.

Pea tiptoed downstairs to politely suggest that she turn it down out of respect for poor departed Bubbles.

Mum, Clover and Tinkerbell were all in the kitchen, perched side by side on the table with the lights off.

'Why are you—?' began Pea.

'Shhh,' whispered Clover urgently, putting her finger to her lips.

Mum beckoned her forward, and Pea stepped closer, seeing at once.

Klaudia's bedroom door was wide open, one single bare lightbulb glowing brightly, the shouty music pumping out. Inside was a whirl of activity. The carpet was strewn with paper, paint pots and scraps of fabric. In the midst of it all was Klaudia, swaying on one leg to the music, a crutch in one hand, a fat paintbrush in the other. In front of her stood her rickety old wardrobe, the doors flung wide open and everything emptied from inside. She was frantically painting the doors in a familiar purple leopard-printed pattern. When they were completely covered, she cast the paintbrush down and grabbed an old cushion, which spewed feathers into the air as she slit it open with a pair of scissors. The feathers got stuck in her hair and landed in the paint – but Klaudia waved the cushion over her head, scattering them in an even wider arc, her eyes shining.

'You'd shout at me if I painted my wardrobe,' muttered Tinkerbell.

'Yes, I would,' said Mum. 'But that's because

you wouldn't have asked first, would you?'

'I thought she was doing a self-portrait?' whispered Pea.

'She is,' said Mum.

'She looks so *free*,' murmured Clover reverently, as Klaudia began to dab paint inside the wardrobe with her fingertips, the air around her still thick with tiny floating feathers.

'Isn't it brilliant? Bubbles did just what you wanted, after all,' whispered Mum, passing Pea an old yellow Post-it note.

Dear Mum of Pea,
I am going to stay with
Klaudia for a little while,
because she needs artistic
inspiration . . .

It was true, Pea thought. Klaudia had worried that her inspiration had dribbled out from the
crack in her bones.

Now, it seemed that painting the goldfish bowl
had filled her back up again.

CHAPTER 9

PEA ON THE PITCH

'But how are you going to do funraisin for the KFC now?' said Tinkerbell crossly, jabbing a finger at the question mark on Pea's CV.

'I don't know,' mumbled Pea unhappily.

'Stinkerbell, we've talked about this,' said Mum. 'Not everyone's life has to revolve around trying to buy a minibus. And no, you still can't sell fake *Mermaid Girls* books with my made-up titles on Amazon. Or my unfinished manuscript. Or a lock of my hair. You can sell home-made chocolate crispy treats at the next Kites match like a normal, sensible fundraiser, all right?'

It was Monday morning. Usually Klaudia was in charge of weekday breakfasts, but Mum had declared that an artist shouldn't have to stop creating just to make toast – 'unless she's me, obviously.' Tinkerbell was eating peanut butter out of the jar and Pea was eating Sugar Puffs when Clover tripped into the kitchen, looking rather unusual.

'What have you *done*?' said Mum, dropping the butter knife.

'Nothing,' said Clover defensively as she poured herself some tea. 'Just a little bit of make-up, that's all. I bought it with my money from Willem. Models always wear make-up.'

That was true, Pea knew. But she was also sure that models usually looked less orange. Clover's cheeks were tinted red in two powdery spots, like a doll's face. Her eyes, however, were pure panda.

'You look like an alien,' said Tinkerbell. 'An alien who needs a wash. Well, she does,' she added, seeing Mum's frown and reaching for more toast.

Mum plucked the toast out of her hand and

held it over her head, pointedly, till Tinkerbell apologized.

'I should think so,' said Clover, jutting her chin out so that the sharp line across her neck where the orange stopped and she went back to normal pinkish Clover-colour was even more noticeable. 'I can't help it if I'm more mature and sophisticated than you are.'

Klaudia hopped out of her little room off the kitchen on her crutches. Her hair was still studded with fluffy white feathers, and she was yawning, but there was a beaming grin on her face.

'Hey! You guys, I swear, last night, it was like a *door* just, like, opened, and—' She broke off mid-sentence to stare at Clover. She blinked, twice. 'I'll have breakfast later,' she said, and hopped back into her bedroom.

'Is it that bad?' whispered Clover, her lower lip trembling.

'Oh, Clover – no, flower,' said Mum soothingly. 'Only, it's a little bit too much for daytime. Or

191

anywhere, really. You are only thirteen, my pixie. You've got lovely skin already – you don't need to cover it up.'

'Thirteen's old enough for make-up!' protested Clover. 'Honey and Tash wear it every day, and they aren't even models.'

'Neither are you today, sweetness – and you won't be one ever again if it's going to turn you into some horrible tantrumming version of my lovely Clover. I'm not having this much drama on a Monday, not when I've got a chapter full of rotting old mermaid legs to write this morning.' Mum looked stern. 'Go and wash your face now, or I'll call Willem and tell him you're sending the money back.'

'But . . . but you can't! I've told everyone at school!'

'Better be quick, then,' said Mum.

Clover thundered upstairs, a single black mascara tear streaking a path down her orange cheek.

'Teenagers – ugh. Do you promise to stay eleven for ever, Pea-nut?' moaned Mum.

'I'll try,' said Pea. 'Are you really writing about rotting mermaid legs?'

Mum nodded, looking miserable. 'I know. Horrible, isn't it? I put all these nasty sea monsters in at the end of book four so there could be an exciting cliffhanger, but now I've got to write about their cave full of skeletons – and I think mermaid skeletons look like people skeletons, don't you?'

Pea nodded queasily. She made Mum her Special Writing Tea in her favourite spotty WE ♥ MUM mug. Then she and a very clean-faced Clover got the bus to school. Clover spent most of the journey reapplying the orange stuff to her face, while Pea reluctantly held up a small mirror. They went over some speed bumps when she was doing the eyeliner, which made Clover look quite surprised in her left eye, but it was too late to start again, so Clover licked her finger and smudged both eyes into extra-panda mode.

'I'll tell everyone I'm being gothic and bohemian – it'll be fine,' Clover said confidently as she strode into Greyhope's.

All morning, Pea thought about her question mark. If only she could go back to her first plan and be like Mum: Marina Cove, who spent her days making up stories – even ones with rotting legs in . . .

But another lesson with Mr Ellis soon got rid of that dream. Pea's one-minute speech on 'Spain' was even worse than her one about Owls. The Llewellyns were an unusually well-travelled family, but they'd never been to Spain, and it turned out not to be the one shaped like a boot. After that unfortunate start Pea never fully recovered.

Mr Ellis gave her 1 out of 5 (though Pea had an uncomfortable feeling he wanted to give her a 0, really).

'I only got one too,' whispered Molly, by way of consolation. Her effort on the subject of 'Cheese' had been mainly a list: cream cheese; cream cheese with chives in; cream cheese with onions in; that one with the cow on the box. Dairylea had featured at least four times.

'It's all right for you – you've always been rubbish at English,' said Pea, without thinking.

Molly went pink. So did Pea.

'I'm so sorry! I didn't mean . . . !'

Molly was very understanding once Pea had explained all about Bubbles, and the question mark, over packed lunches with Bethany.

'You'll think of something to be soon,' said Molly. 'It's not as if it's urgent.'

'But it is!' protested Pea. 'You all know what you want to be. What if I realize I want to be something you have to start practising for when you're really young, like a concert pianist? I could've left it too late already!'

'Do you want to be a concert pianist?' asked Bethany, eating a cheesy Wotsit.

Pea shook her head.

'Well, what are you *good* at?' asked Molly.

Reading, and writing stories, thought Pea – but if that were true, she'd have won the *Spark!* competition, and Mr Ellis would think she was brilliant.

'I don't know,' she said. 'I'm not sure I'm good at anything.'

Seeing the usual cluster of Year Nines waiting outside Mr Ellis's door at the end of lunch time didn't help.

'But he's so mean!' whispered Bethany. 'Why do they like him?'

Pea couldn't fathom it, either – but there they were, giggling to each other about his earring, and his scruffly beard, and the way his long hair flicked about when he rubbed the whiteboard clean.

'And what have they done to their faces?' whispered Molly.

Pea looked closer, and spotted Tash and Honey, both with gothic and bohemian smudgy eyes which she was sure hadn't looked like that this morning.

Clover came sailing down the corridor and flashed her a smile. 'See? I knew everyone would love my new look. Don't tell Mum, OK?'

And she led the other girls into Mr Ellis's room, proclaiming, 'Good afternoon, sir, how are you today?' in a bright cheery voice.

The next day, orange faces and smudgy eyes began to break out all across the school. Clover held model classes in the playground at lunch, launching herself into a string of unnatural positions ('Laughing while Running', 'Surprised Hands' and, most challenging of all, 'The Helicopter') and offering advice on how not to wobble. By Friday, Acting Deputy Head Mrs King had to hold a special assembly to remind all Greyhope's girls that according to the school rules, make-up was strictly forbidden. But still, the girls' toilets next door to the chemistry lab were rammed with eager faces before home time, all keen to replicate the Clover look for the weekend, and at the bus stop Pea spotted several uniformed girls all standing still as statues in various uncomfortable poses.

'I can't help it if I'm influential,' said Clover

airily on the bus home. 'I can do your face next week too, if you like?'

Pea knew she was trying to be kind – but she shook her head firmly. It wasn't her face that was worrying her.

Saturday morning was one of those bright blue-skied February days: cold, but if you were lucky, you might find a patch of sunlight and really feel it warm up your face for the first time in months. It was, Tinkerbell declared, the perfect weather for the Kensal Rise Kites' next football match.

'It's not raining, that's the main thing,' said Mum, slipping on a drapy scarf and some new earrings (jingly ones, with silver beads and peacock feathers). 'Hopefully a few more people will turn out to watch this time.'

Tinkerbell had spent all morning in the kitchen making chocolate crispy cakes to sell for 20p apiece for the KFC. She was so determined to fill up her old spaghetti-hoops tin with money that she hadn't eaten a single one, even when Mum said she could.

'Even if the Kites lose again, it won't matter,' she said, wiping chocolate off her fingers. 'Sad people like sweet things to cheer them up – so that's at least seven crispy cakes.'

'Twenty p, seven cakes: so that would be how much, Tinky-wink?' asked Mum.

Tinkerbell rolled her eyes. 'It's funraisin, Mum, not maths.'

But Tinkerbell's optimism was short-lived. Dr Paget came over, quite flustered.

'Disaster!' she said. 'We're three players short! They called this morning with various made-up-sounding colds and sneezes. I can't blame them, to be honest. The girls try hard, but it's not much fun, being on the losing team week after week. Anyway, Kara's on the phone to a few friends with girls, but it's not looking good, and poor Sam's frantic. I wondered if you could help?'

Tinkerbell's eyes grew huge. She took a deep breath, then stepped forward, standing up very straight. 'I will play for you,' she said, in a noble-sounding voice.

'Oh, Tink, that's very kind, but you're too young – it's just not allowed,' said Dr Paget, giving her shoulder a pat. 'And Clover's too old. I was thinking of Pea, and perhaps a few of her friends.'

Tinkerbell's head drooped, and she went to sit on the floor with Wuffly.

Pea felt awful. Tinkerbell had wanted to be on the team ever since Sam Two had joined – but Pea didn't care at all. She thought back to all those hours with Clem, sitting on the sofa cheering on Birmingham City. Watching a lot of football when she was six or seven (and, to be honest, mostly with her nose in a book, only looking up when Clem and Tinkerbell started jumping up and down) was not at all the same as playing it. At school they did netball and hockey and gymnastics, never football – and she was no good at any of those, anyway. Pea wasn't a sporty sort of person. She was a comfy, staying-in sort of person. She always had been.

'Will it matter if I'm useless?' asked Pea.

'Not at all!' said Dr Paget. 'It's not like we're going to win, so who cares?'

Mum got on the phone to Bethany, Molly and Eloise's parents at once. No one answered at Eloise's house, but the other two said yes.

Dr Paget whirled off to tell Dr Skidelsky the good news.

Klaudia crutched her way out of her little room to see what all the noise was.

'Sorry!' said Mum. 'We'll leave you in peace soon. How's it going?'

Pea tried peering past Klaudia to see what was happening to the wardrobe self-portrait, but the room was in darkness.

'Good, good,' said Klaudia dreamily. 'Hey, cakes! That's, like, totally what I need!'

She grabbed one, stuck it in her top pocket, and disappeared back into her room.

'Is she going to put a chocolate crispy cake in her art?' asked Pea.

201

'Very possibly,' said Mum.

'She didn't even pay twenty p,' said Tinkerbell, folding her arms and sulking.

Mum sat down with Tinkerbell and had a short, serious talk about doing fundraising for a good cause, and not just because you thought it might help you get onto a football team, or win back a friend who wasn't being very friendly any more. Then she gave Wuffly's ears a good ruffle.

'Now come on, my chickens. The KFC needs us!'

By the time they got there the Kites' opponents, the Hampstead Heathers, were all lined up on the pitch, jogging to keep warm in their matching red shirts and red-and-white socks. Dr Paget was setting up goalposts with Sam One's help. The handful of Kites were huddled in a shivery little group, waiting, while Dr Skidelsky anxiously checked her watch. When she spotted Pea, she smiled and blew her whistle.

A moment later, Molly and Bethany spilled out

of a custard-coloured car, followed by Molly's dad. He had black-framed glasses just like his daughter's, and short bristly grey hair.

'I'll stay and watch, if you don't mind?' he said, sniffing a bit at the lumpy muddy field.

'Please do. Would you like a crispy cake?' asked Tinkerbell.

Molly's dad took two.

'That'll be forty p, please,' said Tinkerbell, shoving the spaghetti hoops tin under his surprised nose and jingling it till he put in a pound. She looked very pleased with herself.

'Sorry,' said Mum. 'And thanks so much for bringing the girls along.'

'I've never done football before,' Bethany admitted.

'I've only played with my cousins,' said Molly, 'and not for ages.'

Pea felt better. At least they could all be useless together.

Dr Skidelsky blew her whistle again, frantically

beckoning the three girls over as the Heathers waited impatiently on the pitch. She introduced Pea, Molly and Bethany to the last remaining Kites – Sam Two, Reema, Sallyanne and Nesh.

They formed a tight circle and bent down to whisper tactics. Nesh had a blue strap looped around her shoulders to show that it was her turn to be captain, but it was Sam Two who did all the talking.

'Right, girls,' she said, her face unusually serious. 'I watched the Heathers play last week. They're good up front, really good – but their goalie's brain-dead. Take every chance you get, yeah? Reema, you're fast – stay out on the wing and look out for long high passes. Newbies, just . . . um . . . keep your eyes open, and try not to pass to some-one from the other team, OK?'

Pea nodded.

'Come on, then, ladies. Kites, Kites, Kites!'

All the girls put their arms into the middle of the circle, then lifted them up, whooping. Then they ran backwards, cheering, as they took up their positions.

Facing them, the red-shirted Heathers were doing the same, slotting into their set places. Sam Two gestured to a spot on the pitch, pointing out where Pea should start. There was an enormously tall Heather standing in the same spot on the opposite side of the pitch, swinging her arms menacingly. Pea was fairly sure she was supposed to 'mark' her, like in netball. It didn't look like it would be much of a contest.

Pea looked worriedly across the bumpy, lumpy pitch at Molly, who was hopping from one foot to the other, and Bethany, who had somehow ended up in goal. They looked very small and scruffy next to the Heathers in their shiny red shirts.

Dr Skidelsky blew her whistle, and the game began.

The first few minutes were a blur. Pea was so busy concentrating on marking the enormous girl that she forgot to look for the ball, so when it bounced off the top of her head, conveniently leapfrogging the opposition and rolling remarkably close to the goal, she didn't really feel she could take much credit. Sam Two and Reema charged after it, both spotting that the Heathers goalie was reading a text message and not paying any attention at all – but a red-and white-socked foot reached it first, just in time, and booted it back over all their heads.

The next time the ball came her way, Pea was more ready for it. It landed at her feet, then veered suddenly to the left as it rolled into a bumpy bit of grass. The enormous girl swung at it, missed, and fell over. Pea leaped forward and gave the ball the biggest, hardest thump with her trainer toe that she could muster.

The ball flew up high.

It sailed over the heads of four red-shirted Heathers.

It began to dip, and dip, and then it bounced once, rolled over the shoes of the goalie (who was still reading her texts), and came to a stop just beyond the goal line.

Dr Skidelsky blew her whistle. 'Goal!'

Pea stood still with her mouth open. Then she was engulfed in cheering Kites.

'Go Pea!' yelled Tinkerbell from the touchline, hopping up and down.

'That was amazing!' shouted Molly.

'Well done, newbie!' called Nesh.

Sam Two was looking her up and down with new curiosity.

'It was luck,' mumbled Pea, embarrassed. 'I was lucky.'

But as the game went on, Pea started to realize that it was more than just luck. When the ball began to move from player to player, she was already thinking ahead, working out which Heather it would be passed to next – so she could slip into its path and intercept it. When Sam Two began an urgent run from the centre spot, she was already sprinting far ahead, ready for the long overhead. When Reema spotted the Heathers goalie doing up her shoelaces, Pea sped past Nesh in case she missed Reema's pass. She still stumbled on the lumpy grass or misjudged her kicks so that the ball bounced too far or fell short. But all those hours watching from the sofa with Clem, glancing up from her book, had given her an understanding of the game. She could read it like a story. Each passage of play was like a chapter, ending with an exciting dash for the goal. There were goodies and baddies. There were brilliant moments (that goal, *her* goal) and shocks – like when the enormously tall Heather came running up behind Pea and knocked her flying face-first into the mud – and a quest, a desperate thing to be achieved before time ran out: to win. Only instead of reading the story or writing it, she was *in* it. It was incredibly exciting.

By half-time the score was 2–2.

Pea had mud in her ponytail and couldn't quite catch her breath, but she didn't care. She ran off the pitch alongside her team, feeling like she was glowing from the inside. She was part of something. She was *good* at something.

'You dark horse!' said Dr Skidelsky. 'Where have you been hiding?'

'I can't believe it.' Mum stared at Pea as if she might not really be Pea at all. 'Oh, that sounds awful, sorry. I didn't mean . . . It's just that my Pea-nut's so clever and brainy and sensible. I didn't think you even liked football.'

'Me neither,' giggled Pea, glowing even brighter at being clever and brainy and sensible as well as someone who had scored a goal, right over there, without even properly meaning to. 'I suppose I just haven't really played it before.'

'You were *so* good,' said Nesh.

Even Sam Two shrugged her shoulders and gave Pea a respectful nod. 'Yeah, I see some potential,' she said stiffly.

Tinkerbell went round everyone – Heathers included – with her crispy cakes and the spaghetti-hoops tin, and a rather fierce expression that was hard to say no to. Molly's dad ended up buying sixteen of them. Molly, Bethany and Pea helped him eat them. Then Dr Skidelsky blew the whistle. Half-time was over. It was time for the story to go on.

The second half was every bit as thrilling as the first. Pea's second goal flew past the ear of the ever-texting Heathers goalie within the first two minutes: 3–2.

But a tall brown-haired Heather equalized a moment later, then got a free kick not far from goal. Both times Bethany's fingers got near the ball, but it sailed over her head.

The Heathers were now 4-3 up, with ten minutes to go.

The Heathers swapped a few fresh players onto the field, but with no reserves on the bench, the Kites were forced to carry on, tired legs and all. It only spurred Pea on. They were valiant underdogs, battling tough odds . . . They were the unlikely raggle-taggle heroes, up against shiny-armoured minibus-riding fiends . . .

The ball bounced up awkwardly, and she had to fight the temptation to catch it like a netball, clenching her fists and letting it rebound off her chest. It bounced up again, then rolled through Molly's legs, directly to Sam Two – who flicked it expertly past another Heather, and kicked it long and hard, directly into the top right corner of the goal.

4–4.

Level, with only a few minutes left.

Pea felt her T-shirt sticking to her back, and her nose was running. Molly's glasses were steamed up with sweat. Bethany looked utterly terrified whenever the ball came anywhere near. Sam Two swapped Sallyanne into goal and put Bethany in midfield.

'One minute remaining!' shouted Dr Skidelsky, looking at her stopwatch.

They were so close.

When the ball next landed at her feet, Pea didn't hesitate. She kept it close, made sure her giant marker was behind her, and wove round the bumps of turf. She passed to Nesh. Nesh passed to Reema. Reema stumbled but recovered, and passed back to Pea. The Heathers goalie wasn't texting this time, but Pea was determined to get past her all the same. She kept the ball at her feet, steered it round a mushy puddle of mud, made as if to kick – then, at the last moment, changed direction, tapped it on one more time, and let it fly.

The Heathers goalie went one way.

The ball went the other.

'GOAL!' yelled Tinkerbell.

The whistle blew three times. It was 5–4 to the Kites, and Pea had scored the winning goal.

'We won!' yelled Sam Two, sprinting around the pitch with her arms spread out like a plane.

'We won!' howled Dr Skidelsky, throwing her whistle in the air and performing a most uncharacteristic cartwheel.

'We made loads of money for the KFC!' yelled Tinkerbell, jingling the spaghetti-hoops tin over her head.

The other Kites were all as muddy and ex-hausted as Pea was, but she could see how thrilled they were. 'You will join the Kites properly, won't you?' said Reema.

Nesh looked pleading. 'We've got the Ruislip Rockets next, and they're *mean*. We haven't got a hope without you!'

Pea beamed. 'I'd love to.'

She could feel Sam Two watching her out of the corner of her eye, and thought she noticed a glare from under her floppy brown hair. But a moment later she was shaking Pea's hand and smiling.

'Yeah, great, Pea. Good to have you on the team.'

If Tinkerbell was jealous of Pea's success, she hid it very well.

'We haven't quite got enough for a minibus

yet, but I think we'll be able to buy matching socks soon,' she said, still clutching her tin.

'Not that you needed them,' said Dr Paget proudly.

'Oh no. We're going to have to make chocolate crispy cakes for every match now, aren't we?' moaned Mum.

'They are delicious, mind,' said Molly's dad, through a chocolaty mouthful.

'Dad, how many of those have you had?' asked Molly.

Bethany and Molly and Molly's dad came back for a cup of tea and more crispy cakes – free ones – as a thank-you.

Pea nodded along to their conversations, but her mind was still on the pitch, reliving that flying sensation in her chest when the ball bounced into the goal. The moment Molly's dad drove her friends off in his custard-coloured car, she went directly to the kitchen and, her hand still streaked with mud, grabbed a pencil.

PEA

Age: 11

Current occupation: schoolgirl

Likes: books

Special skills: writing, reading,
   making sandwiches

Future career: ~~writer (like Mum)~~ ?

   ~~pet therapist~~ ?

   footballer

CHAPTER 10

DRIP DRIP DRIP

'Here you are, Klaudia!' yelled Pea, dropping another set of muddy football-practice clothes on top of the washing machine.

'Er . . . thanks? Do you, like, *have* to want to be a footballer?' said Klaudia, wrinkling her nose. 'I thought old chocolaty-trousers over there was bad enough.'

Tinkerbell beamed stickily from the kitchen table as she scooped yet another batch of crispy cakes into paper cases. Her head teacher had been persuaded to let her sell them at lunch times, and the house now smelled constantly of melty chocolate. For the first few days it had been lovely to come home to from school, but now it made Pea feel a bit sick.

Not that she was spending much time at home.

Almost every afternoon, the moment she got back from school, she threw off her Greyhope's uniform, pulled on trackie bottoms and trainers, and hurried next door to meet Sam Two for football practice. Sam Two was as quick-tempered and shouty as ever – even more so after Dr Skidelsky had let slip that Pea was quite the best player in the Kites now – but she wanted to win so much she even let Tinkerbell come over occasionally, to be goalie for penalty practice. Sam One would peep out from time to time to ask if Pea might not prefer to come and help with *Space Ant vs. the Electric Merman*, or to have orange juice and biscuits – and quite often Pea's legs were tired, and Sam Two had yelled something rude at her, and she really did quite want to say yes – but she knew where she needed to be. Football was her new future.

Even if she was naturally brilliant at it (truly, the ball sometimes seemed attached to her toes by an invisible string), she still had to make sacrifices.

It was wonderful, Pea thought, to feel so sure about herself. This must be what Clover felt like all the time.

As February became March, and the days grew brighter and sunnier, the whole family seemed to be on an upward swing. Mum's next book was, she said, 'flying along at last'. She and the fearsome Dreaditor had finally agreed on a title – *Snowflake Island* – and once that was settled, the words followed. Pea noticed that she still spent rather more time drawing pirate ships than writing about them, and the WE ♥ MUM Special Writing Mug had vanished somewhere, which was a worry – but she seemed happy.

Klaudia went to see the doctor, who took off her purple-strapped leg cast and gave her a new one wrapped in orange plastic stuff that she was allowed to walk on, though she still had crutches.

218

'My own leg is so totally disgusting,' she said, gleefully showing them a photo on her phone, taken in between plasters. One leg looked quite normal, but the broken one was pale and skinny, and very hairy.

Klaudia got her college friend Aimee to cut her faded hair short again. All the leopard-printiness was gone – but with Clover's help, Klaudia re-dyed it in tiger stripes, orange and black to match her new cast. The doctor had said she was supposed to exercise more, and Wuffly definitely needed to (all those weeks of apple pie and limping had left her looking quite podgy), so they would disappear off to the charity shop round the corner together, returning with the oddest selection of 'art supplies': plastic dolls' heads, broken picture frames, velvet cushions with rips in. Pea couldn't fathom how any of these would turn a wardrobe into a self-portrait. It was still locked away in Klaudia's bedroom, and none of them – not even Tinkerbell – had dared to peep.

Clover's modelling future, meanwhile, seemed more secure than ever. If Clover wore a heart-shaped beauty mark on her cheek, or her hair in plaits looped up by her ears like a milkmaid, by lunch time so did half of Year Nine. So when Willem called to let her know that one of her pictures had been bought by Angelhair shampoo for a magazine advert, she simply smiled down the phone and said, 'Of course it has!'

From then on, Clover drifted through the corridors of Greyhope's with an imaginary halo already hovering above her golden locks, announcing to her flock of followers that she was 'the face of Angelhair shampoo' and promising them all free samples. (Pea didn't think this was such a good idea after trying the bottle Clover had rushed out to buy. It made her thick red hair even more frizzy than usual, and left it smelling very strongly of lemons – not in a delicious refreshing lemonade way, either; more like washing-up liquid.)

Clover was a model. Tink was a 'funraisin'. Pea

– who scored six of the Kites' nine goals against the Ruislip Rockets, taking them into the semi-finals of the North and West London Junior Girls' League – was most definitely a footballer.

It was nearly springtime, and everything behind their raspberry-red front door was quite, quite perfect.

At least, Pea felt it *ought* to be. Yes, Klaudia did still play German shouting music very loudly a lot of the time. Clover had become quite boring to talk to unless you said things about hair. Tinkerbell had ruined chocolate. Mr Ellis's English lessons were still horrible; Pea lay awake at night fretting over his flashing blue eyes and his gold earring – before dropping off to nightmare Oral Presentations in which she unfolded her slip of paper to read MY MOST EMBARRASSING MOMENT, and had to fill her minute with the tale of that time her school skirt got tucked into her knickers and no one told her for ages. And she did feel a tiny bit guilty about replacing Sam Two as 'Best Kite'. But something else was wrong. She had a sort of slow, dripping feeling of unease, as if it were raining inside her head.

'Maybe you've got a horrible brain disease,' said Molly, at school.

'Um,' said Pea, alarmed. 'I don't think it's that. I mean, it's not *actually* raining inside my head.'

Bethany rubbed Pea's hair, as if to check for dampness, and nodded. Then she frowned and sniffed her hand. 'Can anyone else smell washing-up liquid?' she asked.

Pea shook her head, and secretly resolved to throw away Clover's Angelhair shampoo the minute she got home.

But still it went on, the feeling: *drip drip drip*, in the back of her mind.

What could possibly be making her feel so unhappy? It wasn't until the Kites' semi-final match against the Finchley Goldfinches that Pea began to understand.

It was a cloudy Saturday with swirly wind.

Molly's dad drove the Kites, in batches, to Finchley, where the pitch was perfectly flat and no one had to worry about goalposts falling over.

Once again, Pea played brilliantly. Sam Two's tactics were perfectly judged against a team that were quick on their feet but lacked a strong finisher. They made spectacular long passes – but they were predictable, and after the first few it became easier to intercept them, and turn the game round in a heartbeat. Pea could read it all. The game was a book, the familiar chapters stacking up in sequence.

And that, at last, was the final *drip* in Pea's head.

It was boring.

It was a story she'd already read.

Someone kicked a ball – and it went in the goal, or it didn't. Pass, tackle, whistle, corner. It was the same thing, over and over. It didn't matter that she was the best in the team. However much she wanted to help the Kites win – for Sam Two, for Tinkerbell, for Dr Skidelsky running madly up and down the pitch – it wasn't fun. It was like waiting at the doctor's when you'd forgotten to bring a book. It was like sitting in the back of a car, being told off for asking 'Are we nearly there yet?' while grown-ups frowned at maps. It was like listening to Clover talk about shampoo.

Pea might be good enough to be a football star – but it didn't make her heart sing. It wasn't what she wanted.

When the whistle blew, the Kites had beaten the Goldfinches 4–3.

'We did it! We did it!' Sam Two yelled, dragging Pea into a huddle of whooping, cheering girls.

'You did it, you did it! You're in the final!' yelled Dr Skidelsky, flinging her arms around them too.

Pea smiled and jumped and cheered with all the rest – but inside her head there was nothing but a steady drizzle.

The question, now, was what to do about it.

Pea waited until that night after tea to talk to

Mum. Mum had understood at once why Pea couldn't be a pet therapist after what happened with Bubbles. She'd understand this too.

She found Mum in the kitchen, on the phone to Clem. Whenever he rang, the sisters usually took turns to say hello and tell him all their news – but instead of passing the phone to Pea, she hung up.

'Great news, girls!' she yelled, clapping her hands together. 'Clem's coming to visit!'

Tinkerbell grinned. 'It's because he's heard about my chocolate crispy cakes,' she told Pea proudly.

'And my advert,' said Clover, tossing her hair. (She wore it down every day now, and perfectly tousled around her shoulders 'like real angels do', though no one was quite sure how she knew this.)

'*Yes*,' said Mum. 'Those things too. And just to see us. But once he heard about the Kites being in the final next weekend . . .'

'You mean . . .' said Pea, in a small voice, 'he's coming to London specially to watch me play?'

225

Mum stroked Pea's ponytail fondly, and nodded. 'Isn't it wonderful? He's so proud. Of all of you,' she added quickly, but Pea knew what she meant. Clem loved football just as much as Sam Two did. He'd be thrilled she was in the team.

Pea went upstairs and climbed into bed with all her clothes still on. The *drip drip drip* in her head was now a positive downpour. There was simply no way she could tell Mum she didn't like football now.

The week passed miserably for Pea. Mr Ellis gave her a zero for her near-silent Oral Presentation on 'Hedgerows', and another for her grammar test on *subjects* and *objects* in sentences (which was fair, as Pea had absent-mindedly underlined every single word). Every day after school, Sam Two would come knocking to demand a kickabout.

Everyone else was giddily excited. Clover hunted for her advert in every magazine at the big Tesco, while Klaudia and Tinkerbell went to buy seven cheap yellow T-shirts. The rest of the week was spent laboriously cutting out letters from blue felt and gluing the Kites' names onto the backs. (Pea's said PEA instead of LLEWELLYN, because no one wanted to cut out that many Ls.)

By Friday, Tinkerbell was beside herself.

'Can we make profiteroles for the KFC this time instead of crispy cakes, Klaudia? Can we do caramel ones? Dad likes caramel. Can we make him a Kensal Rise Kites team shirt too? I bet he'd like one. We could glue his name on it, even though he's not a Kite. I'll cut out the letters.'

Saturday morning arrived at last: a clear mid-March day with bright blue skies. Pea was already wide awake, staring at the ceiling, when the bell rang just after seven a.m.

It was Sam Two on the doorstep, already in her yellow Kites shirt (with PAGET-SKIDELSKY hand-sewn on the back by Dr Paget), running on the spot. Her eyes were huge, with little grey handbags underneath them.

'Can't sleep,' she said breathlessly, arms pumping. 'Need to practise. Got to win.'

Pea nodded grimly, and went upstairs to change. The yellow shirt was scratchy, and made her look ill under her red hair.

By the time Dr Skidelsky took them down to the lumpy old field, Pea was more sick of football than she'd ever been. She hoped Sam Two's enthusiasm might be infectious, but as the kick-off drew closer, Sam Two's eyes got wider and her tactical pep-talks more high-pitched and breathless, until Dr Skidelsky had to take her to one side for a calming glass of water and a dry biscuit.

'Don't let the pressure get to you, girls,' Dr Skidelsky said, leading a swaying Sam Two back to the team. 'Obviously we'd all really, really, *really* like to win—' She broke off, looking rather baggy-eyed too. Then she shook herself. 'But it's a game. You're here to have fun. Just play your best, yes? Your very, very best.'

Pea felt Dr Skidelsky's eyes behind their oblong glasses focus in on her, and she swallowed hard.

The playing field was as muddy and puddly as

ever – but today there was a small crowd of spectators, who gave them a cheer as they ran over the
hill. Tinkerbell and Mum had set up a proper stall
for their crispy cakes. From somewhere Dr Paget
had found a big silver urn, and was making cups of
warmish tea in polystyrene cups for 50p; Sam One
was on sugar duty. And clapping furiously on the
touchline, wearing his Birmingham City bobble
hat and scarf, was Clem.

'Hey, how's my little superstar?' he said, sweeping Pea up in a hug.

'All right,' mumbled Pea, feeling suddenly shy.

It was silly, she knew; it was Clem, *their* Clem,
even if she hadn't seen him since Christmas. But
he'd grown a funny little mini-beard under his
bottom lip, and his hair was curling around his ears
under his hat, and somehow he didn't match the
Clem in her head.

He was frowning at her, as if he were thinking
the same thing. 'Are you sure about that?' he said,
dropping down into a crouch to see her face better.

Pea clutched her thumbs and nodded as hard as she could, even though the *drip drip dripping* feeling was stronger than ever.

Clem's eyes narrowed. 'Right, come on,' he said, gripping her elbow and steering her off to a quiet spot. They sat side by side on the muddy grass. 'Don't fuss about all that lot – they can wait. Now tell me the truth, pet. What's up? What's going on in that busy old head of yours, eh?'

Pea bit her lip. Then she took a deep breath. '*I don't like football,*' she said, in a whisper.

Clem cracked a smile. 'Is that all? Well, I knew *that.*'

Pea blinked.

'You never did like it,' he continued. 'Your mum used to go nuts with me when she found out I'd stuck you on the sofa in front of the game all afternoon. Tink got right into it, but you and Clover? Just wasn't your cup of tea. When I started hearing you were playing in matches and going off training – well, don't get me wrong, I was chuffed . . .

230

but, to be honest, I did wonder.'

'But I'm really *good* at it,' said Pea, in a guilty whisper.

'So?'

'So that's what I should do. It says so on my CV.'

Clem chuckled, and stroked his funny little mini-beard. 'Is this why I haven't been getting any emails from you lately? Too busy planning your lifetime career to write to little old me?'

Pea blushed. 'Sort of. I've got this English teacher, and . . . well, you don't need to hear about that.' (Clem was very good at some Dad-like things, but he'd never cared very much about doing well at school; he wouldn't understand.) 'I tried doing some other things – Wuffly broke her leg, and then there was a fish, only . . .' Pea tailed off. It was all quite hard to explain to someone who hadn't been there.

'Pea?' asked Clem, putting on his almost-serious face. 'Do you want to play football?'

Pea shook her head very hard.

Clem's face broke into a big broad smile. 'Then you don't have to, petal. It's not like going to the dentist. It's a hobby. If it's making you sad, stop.'

'Really?' whispered Pea.

'*Really.*'

Pea guessed she must still have looked doubtful, because Clem gave her nose a friendly *honk* between finger and thumb, like he used to back when Tinkerbell was a tiny baby.

'But what about the match?' she asked, looking down at her special yellow T-shirt.

Clem looked out across the field, where the other footballers were already lined up. Dr Skidelsky was staring over at them, looking nervous.

'How long is this final?'

'Twenty minutes each way. With ten minutes in the middle for squash and an orange.'

Clem nodded thoughtfully. 'Well, I reckon the Pea I know would put up with forty minutes of something a bit boring rather than let everybody down. In fact, she'd probably play her best football ever. And then she'd wait for just the right moment, and explain that she was retiring from her glittering football career. What do you think?'

The *drip drip drips* blew away like a cloud in a windy sky.

'There's one condition, though,' Clem went on, now looking very serious indeed.

Pea's stomach clenched up, just like it did before Oral Presentations.

'I want my weekly emails back. Every single week, now – no slacking.'

Pea smiled in relief. 'With bullet points?'

'Course – they're the best bit!' said Clem.

Then he clapped his big jumpery arm round her shoulder, and they walked back to the pitch together.

Pea saw Mum mouthing questions at Clem, her brow all crinkly, but he winked and whispered in her ear. Giving Pea an encouraging tug of her frizzy ponytail, he peeled away, lifted Tink up onto his shoulders, and began yelling, 'Go Kites! Go Kites!'

Pea ran onto the pitch to join the other yellow shirts. Sam Two was now practically green in the face with terror – but Clem's cheerful chanting (even Molly's dad was joining in) seemed to shake her back to herself, and she beckoned them into the pre-match huddle.

'Now, three-two-one – overheads – keep the ball moving. We can do it. We can do it. Can we?' Sam Two's green-tinged face tilted towards Pea, all her usual confidence wilting.

'*Definitely*,' said Pea.

Sam Two took a deep breath. 'You know what? I think we really can. Yes! *Come on, Kites!*'

The Kites fanned out across the pitch.

The whistle blew, and the game was on.

'Now, you mustn't be too disappointed, girls,' said Dr Paget when they reached the red-brick pillar at the end of the Paget-Skidelskys' drive. 'It's amazing you even made the final. And you all played your socks off.'

They had played the felt letters on their yellow T-shirts off too; every now and then Pea would spot one fluttering past, having come unglued. It hadn't been enough to distract the Highgate Harriers, though. A 7–2 defeat. Not even close.

'Yeah,' murmured Sam Two from under her floppy hair.

'Yeah,' murmured Dr Skidelsky, in exactly the same unpersuaded tone.

'I liked the bit where the ball bounced off Bethany's bottom best,' said Tinkerbell brightly.

'Tink!' said Clem and Mum, both at once – but even Dr Skidelsky snorted at that.

Pea caught Clem's eye, and smiled a proper full smile that stretched across her face. It would have been brilliant to have won her last ever match, the perfect end to her footballing story. But she didn't mind, not like Sam Two did.

They waved goodbye to the Paget-Skidelskys

and walked up the crazy-paving path. Pea had only one thing on her mind: updating her CV.

She left Mum, Tinkerbell and Clem to flop on the sofa, and hurried into the kitchen, wincing at Klaudia's loud shouty music – but as she picked up a pencil to cross out *footballer*, her eye fell on Clover's CV. Where it had once read *model*, there was now a scribbling-out so fierce it had torn the paper and scribbled on the fridge underneath.

Over the thumping bass from Klaudia's room, Pea heard a desperate sob.

She turned round. Clover was crumpled up behind the table, Wuffly's podgy tummy clutched in her arms, a magazine open on the floor beside her.

'Oh Pea!' wailed Clover. 'It's the end of the world!'

It only took a moment for Pea to understand. The long-awaited advert for Angelhair shampoo had appeared in a magazine at last. It showed the faces of two girls side by side, as if they were looking in a bathroom mirror. One smiling girl had beautiful blonde hair, styled smooth and shiny, and a glowing halo around her head – but it was a photograph of some other model. The picture of Clover was the contrasting girl, with hair all fluffy, *before* using Angelhair shampoo. They'd even given her head two little horns, and put red dots in her eyes. Worst of all, otherwise it looked exactly like Clover always did: pleasantly tousled. Pretty. But – according to the advert – too ordinary to be an angel.

'Help me, Pea!' sobbed Clover. 'What am I going to do?'

THE QUESTION MARK

Dear Clem,

Here is all our news.

• Clover has stopped crying (mostly). She did try to cut off all her hair, but she used Tink's scissors, which are rubbish, so there was just a sort of clumpy part missing on one side. Klaudia's friend Aimee gave her a new haircut which looks exactly the same to me. Clover says it's very, very different, though.

• Tink got Mum to take her to ALL the news-agents in Kensal Rise and all the ones by school, and she used her KFC money to buy every magazine that had the Angelhair shampoo advert in. Clover didn't ask her to or anything. That made Mum cry, but in the nice way.

• So far no one at school seems to have seen the advert, but Clover is still wearing a hat and sunglasses in the daytime just in case.

• I have given Tinkerbell my Kites T-shirt. She is wearing it as her nightie now.

• Now the KFC tin is empty, Tink is inventing new fundraising ideas. So far 'ice sculpture' is not working out as it means taking all the drawers out of the freezer (even if they have fish fingers in them). Mum is trying to persuade her to take Wuffly out for sponsored runs instead. (You were right, she is a bit fat now from breaking her leg, but we try not to say it in front of her because it makes her sad. I learned this when I was nearly a pet therapist.)

• I am much happier now I'm not trying to be a footballer (thank you!), but I'm not sure what I'll be now. I am trying not to worry.

- Trying not to worry is quite difficult.

We miss you already. Come back soon?
Love from Pea xx
P.S. I'm really really sorry for stopping sending emails. I missed writing them.

Now that she wasn't kicking a ball around next door's garden, Pea had much more time to spend with Sam One. They would meet up after school and sit at Pea's kitchen table or in Sam One's bedroom. Pea had missed having him around to talk to as well; he was calming and sensible, and much less likely to cry or set fire to things than anyone in her own family.

Sam One was working on a new comic called *Spaceship: Kolkokron*. Pea was still determined not to help out with the words (Mr Ellis had deemed her write-up of the Kites vs. Harriers match 'an over-written and implausible failure' as non-fiction, which seemed unfair about a thing that had really happened) – but luckily a comic set in space meant lots of scenes with black backgrounds dotted with little stars. Pea thought even she could manage those.

When Sam One came round on Thursday after school, Pea asked Klaudia for some black paint. Klaudia passed it out through a tiny crack in her bedroom door, then slammed it again without a word. Music – not the German shouty kind; lately it had been whale song and panpipes, which to be honest no one thought was much of an improvement – floated from behind the door. Klaudia's self-portrait would go on display at the art college in only one week's time, and still no one had laid eyes on it.

'So if you aren't going to be a footballer,' said Sam One, drawing a big curly alien like a woodlouse, 'what are you going to be?'

'I don't know,' said Pea, feeling flat. 'I think I might ask Molly what a molecular geneticist does. I'm pretty sure you wear a lab coat and squirt things into test tubes. I could probably do that.'

Sam One sniffed. 'Doesn't sound very creative. You should do something arty, even if it's not writing. I mean, you've still got lots of storyish thoughts, right? They've got to go somewhere.'

Pea's hand wobbled as she painted some more black space, and the brush went over Sam One's neatly pencilled edge. It was tricky trying to go round all the tiny white stars without painting over their points too.

'Sorry,' she said, feeling Sam One's disappointment at her spoiling his drawing, even though he hadn't said anything. 'Well, I'm definitely not going to be an artist.'

'What?' In a waft of panpipes, Klaudia appeared, hobbling on one crutch. 'Anyone can be an artist! Just takes a bit of – you know, inspiration.' She started taking out vegetables for that night's dinner, and peered over Sam One's shoulder.

'Nice strip,' she said. 'Perspective's a bit off here

– you know about vanishing points, right? I've got a book somewhere that'll get you set up. But . . . oh, love love *love* all this.' She waved the potato peeler vaguely at Pea's expanse of space, with its wonky edges and mutant stars. 'It's got flow, yeah? Like you're breaking out of the confines of the medium. Changing the rules. Curves where people expect straight lines, spatter where it's meant to be all pristine clean . . .'

From Sam One's pained expression, Pea could tell that straight lines and pristine clean was more what he'd wanted. Usually she would've agreed. But Klaudia made painting outside the lines sound exciting and new.

Klaudia was definitely the sort of grown-up Pea thought she might like to turn into; someone a bit different. And Sam One had said she should be something creative.

'Klaudia?' said Pea, dipping her paintbrush in the murky pot of water. 'Say I wanted to try being an artist, just to see if I liked it . . . could I come to

243

your drawing class – the one Clover did modelling for that time?'

Klaudia wiped her eyes (she was chopping an onion) and gave Pea a grin. 'Yeah! It's my very last class on Monday. Come along. Both of you, I mean,' she added.

Sam One had been looking rather gloomy, but he cheered up at once at the extra invitation, especially when Dr Paget rang and said he could stay for dinner. They spent the next half-hour cutting up potatoes into crooked star shapes to print new blotchy, silvery stars over the top of Pea's painted sky. Tinkerbell helped, which meant there were a few too many stars, and Mum was a little bit cross that their dinner of sausage and mash turned into sausage and pasta twirls (with onion gravy) instead, but at least she agreed that the comic looked good.

'It doesn't look like the comics in shops,' said Clover, peering over her sunglasses suspiciously as she laid out knives and forks.

'That's the point!' said Klaudia. 'Why make art

that looks like everyone else's? Original, that's what it is.'

Original. Pea liked the sound of that. She grabbed a pencil and darted over to the fridge.

Mum frowned over her shoulder as she updated her CV. 'I can't keep up! You're going to be an artist now, are you?'

'We both are,' said Sam One. 'We're going to go to Klaudia's life-drawing class. You know, Clover, the one where you did modelli—'

With a yelp, Tinkerbell leaped across the table and wrapped her small hand across his mouth. 'We don't say the m-word!' she hissed, looking fearfully at Clover.

Pea braced herself for an eruption of tears – but Clover merely sat down, removed her sunglasses, and pulled a plate of sausages towards her.

'It's quite all right. I don't care about modelling any more. Mrs Sharma says the school Drama Club has utterly fallen apart without me, and *begged* me to come back.'

Pea had been there yesterday when Clover went to see Mrs Sharma, and the begging had all been rather the other way round – but she decided not to say so, and ate a sausage in silence.

The following Monday night, Clover was left in charge of Tinkerbell and Wuffly, and Klaudia, Mum, Sam One and Pea took the two buses to the art college. Pea even borrowed two of Klaudia's floaty scarves. She sat next to Mum (who was wearing three of them: one purple, one orange and spotty, one grey with silvery threads) and felt very artistic indeed.

She *was* going to be just like her mum, after all: the version of her mum who had always wanted to go to art college, and became a writer by accident. It made her glow from the inside out.

Once they were back inside the art school's long, white, overlit halls, Pea felt more certain than ever. Sam One's eyes grew wider and wider as they joined the other students at the circle of easels.

'They're all really grown up,' he whispered, looking anxious, after one of them had shaken his hand.

'I know,' Pea whispered back. 'But don't worry, Klaudia won't be upset if they're better than you.'

Klaudia and Mum were having a secretive discussion about something – which was obviously to do with Pea and Sam One. Then Mum shrugged, and they both giggled, and Klaudia clapped her hands to start the class.

'OK, ladies and gents, let's do this. Life class, yeah? So we're looking at the form of the human body. Our model today is Lena; thank you, Lena.'

Pea shyly took her place in the circle of easels in between Sam One and Mum, who gave her an encouraging smile. Then Lena the model came out: not an Angelhair shampoo sort of model, but quite an old lady with grey hair and crinkly skin, and no clothes on. None. At all. There was a big white sheet on the chair in the middle of the circle, and when she sat down she draped it around herself, but she still wasn't really covered up.

Pea felt her face flush bright, brilliant red. She glanced over at Sam One. He had his eyes shut, very tightly.

'It's only a body, Pea,' whispered Mum, leaning over to pat her hand. 'Klaudia asked if I thought you were old enough for a nude life model, and I told her you were two very mature young people. But if I was wrong, tell me . . .'

Pea looked back at Sam One. He now had one eye open, and was squinting at the model with a look somewhere between horror and fascination.

Pea shook her head. No – a proper artist wouldn't get worried about it. It *was* only a body. And she *did* like the sound of being a mature young person.

Mum had a quick whisper with Sam One, just to check, and then they began to draw.

Lena the model was almost facing Pea, with the sheet draped sideways across her, one bent bare leg sticking out, her head twisted so that her face was in profile. It was a rather good pose, Pea thought (which was a very artistic thing to think, she imagined, and felt encouraged).

But her pencil did not feel the same way.

Pea tried to draw the line of the model's nose, all the way down to her chin – but it was far too small on the huge empty page.

She started again, but this time the nose went pointy like a triangle, and her pencil skidded too low for the chin, so it stuck out like a cartoon witch's.

She sneaked a look at Mum's sketch – which was all charcoal smudges and really quite special-looking. Sam One had started slowly too, but now that he had both his eyes open he was making a very good job of drawing the model's hair. Pea's, by comparison, was hopeless. But by the time she'd rubbed out both attempts, the bell tinkled, and the model shifted to a new pose, facing in a completely new direction with her hands on her hips and her chin tipped up.

All around her, Pea realized the other artists were all flipping over their papers and starting afresh on a new sheet. Hoping no one would notice, she started again on the same page. But this time was no different. Her attempt at shoulders was too small and cramped, and distinctly wonky.

'Sorry – it's a bit harder than I expected,' mumbled Pea when Klaudia came round the circle to see their efforts.

'Mmm,' said Klaudia. 'Try to relax more, yeah? Like, just let the pencil *flow*.'

For the next pose, the model turned away from Pea, and draped one arm over the back of her chair. Poor Pea did her best to let the pencil flow. But the result was not a swooping, clever series of sketchy lines like Mum's, or even a neat, detailed piece in miniature like Sam One's. It looked exactly like what it was: a child's drawing, and not a very good one at that.

Pea couldn't understand it. Her mum could do it. She ate a packed lunch made by a real artist every day. Surely she should have absorbed *some* artistic talent?

Suddenly the big airy studio felt exactly like being in Mr Ellis's classroom, waiting for her turn at Oral Presentations.

Pea sat still and left her paper blank for the last two tinkles of the bell. Mum and Sam One were both too absorbed in their own work to notice. Klaudia didn't even bother to encourage her to try when she came round the circle; she just smiled and patted Pea's shoulder as her nose sank further and further into her loopy scarves. Once the final bell rang and everyone applauded Lena, Pea tugged her single used page from the easel, folded it up and shoved it firmly in her pocket so no one could ask to see.

'Remember how nervous I was, the first class I went to?' said Mum, on the bus home. 'Don't fret, my chick, it does get easier.'

'You'll get better with practice,' said Sam One hopefully.

But Pea wasn't convinced.

They dropped Sam One off next door.

'Mum Gen, I drew a woman with no clothes on!' he shouted as he went in, so Mum had to follow him to explain about her only being mostly naked.

Klaudia and Pea went back home together. Pea waited until she thought Klaudia was comfortably flopped on the sofa with a mug of tea, then tip-toed into the kitchen to bury her folded-up page of shame in the bin.

'Oi! Don't do that!' said Klaudia, who had come back for a biscuit. She grabbed the page from Pea's fingers and spread it out on the kitchen table, smoothing the wrinkles flat.

'It's all right, you don't have to be nice,' said Pea in a small voice. 'I know I can't draw.'

'Well, no, you can't – these are rubbish,' Klaudia agreed.

Pea blinked. She wouldn't have minded Klaudia lying just a *little* bit.

But Klaudia shook her head. 'No, listen: *these* are rubbish. Doesn't mean that *you* are. There's, like, tons of people in that class who can't draw. Duh – that's why they're there! Even on my grad course, some of them can't. Remember that wire horse? The artist worked all that out on a computer. Art isn't only pencils and paper; not just some nice paintings of flowers. I mean, come on!'

She grabbed her one crutch, hopped across the room and flung open her bedroom door.

Pea hung back. 'Your self-portrait . . . Are you sure?'

It had been kept such a secret until now that she couldn't believe Klaudia would let her be the first to see it.

Klaudia grinned, and gave her a little push.

The bedroom wasn't at all like Pea remembered it. When Klaudia first moved in, it had been quite bare, with only a few boxes, a small pile of books, and a fluffy pink rug-like thing on her bed. Now, it was like entering a cave of art. The curtains (sheer fabric, in blues and greens) let in filtered underwatery light. The air was hazy with the smell of paint and glue – and even though music wasn't playing, Pea swore she could still hear faint panpipes.

In the middle of it all stood Klaudia's self-portrait.

Pea knew it had once been a wardrobe, but it seemed to have grown into something entirely new and unnameable. A golden edge, like an old ornate picture frame, was now fixed to the outside. The purple painted doors hung open to reveal soft mounds of fabric within like the seat of a throne, or a magical mountain range: red velvet cushions and bright green sari material, all dusted with tiny white feathers like hills topped with snow, inviting you to climb inside. Pinpricks of white light lit the inside like a starry sky. Beneath, draped over hangers instead of clothes, there were handwritten letters and photographs, little trinkets Klaudia had collected on her travels – even one of Tinkerbell's crispy cakes, dusted with glitter and shiny like a jewel.

'It's not finished yet; I've still got loads of stuff I want to add before it goes on display on Saturday.'

Pea realized she was holding her breath. 'It's beautiful,' she whispered. It was, too – crazy, and strange, and beautiful – and absolutely a self-portrait of Klaudia, even if it didn't show her eyes or her face. Klaudia was right. You could be an artist in so many different ways.

Klaudia grinned, obviously pleased. 'So – could you help me with one thing? My mum and my vati can't come to the showcase, but I promised to send them a video so they can see the piece – and for the coursework, I'm supposed to show my, like, process. You know – sketches and stuff? Only I don't really have any, so I thought I'd just make a film. You can record it on my phone, yeah?'

Pea nodded, proud to be asked to help.

Klaudia handed her the phone – a smart one with a touchscreen like Clem's, with the tiny built-in camera already set up to record. It was rather distracting, seeing a screen that reflected her own face to her as she filmed, but Pea did her best to ignore it. She tapped the icon that made the red light come on, and gave Klaudia the thumbs-up.

Klaudia beckoned her forward to capture the wardrobe in more detail, walking all the way around it, dipping her head inside. As Pea filmed, Klaudia talked – her eyes bright, her hands moving quickly – about the strange little objects that dangled from the hangers (a fortune from a fortune cookie on her twenty-first birthday, an origami frog made by her mother when she was a little girl), and about why she'd chosen to arrange the pieces the way she had. When Klaudia pushed the hangers apart, Pea gasped. The back of the wardrobe was cleverly painted with perspective, so that it seemed to open up into a whole new world. And not just any world: it was their own street under a moonlit night sky, with a bicycle lying on the road, and a raspberry-red front door just visible in the row of houses. There was even a mermaid swimming in a puddle.

Pea was amazed. It was so perfect! And so hidden away! But when Klaudia described it, she talked about perspective, and 'the found art of the doll's house', and why she'd chosen certain kinds of paint and colours, all very technical-sounding, as if she were writing an essay. It was confusing. To Pea, it was like Narnia and Klaudia all rolled into one, with cushions on. But when Klaudia talked about it, it seemed like something much more complicated.

When she was finished, Klaudia dipped into a bow. Pea tapped the screen again, and the red light went off.

'Do you want to watch it now, just to check I did it right?' asked Pea.

Klaudia shook her head. 'No worries – I'm sure it's fine. If there's any problem, I'll get Willem to edit it; he's magic with film stuff.'

Pea nodded slowly, still looking at the revealed

picture of their street hidden in the back panel. There was a lump in her throat.

'Hey, you look sad,' said Klaudia. 'It's not meant to make you sad!'

'I'm not sad, exactly,' said Pea slowly, thinking hard. 'Only – I could never imagine something like this. It's not about whether I can make a pencil draw the right shapes. Even if I could draw properly, I'd never have the ideas. I don't think my brain works in shapes and colours and different directions that way. So . . .' She took a deep breath. 'So I've decided. I don't want to be an artist, after all.'

With a strange sense of loss, she went over to the fridge and crossed out *artist*.

She was a '?' all over again.

CHAPTER
12

WUFFLY

Pea was miserable.

It was the last day of the school term. Five more lessons, then two whole weeks of Easter holidays – which would start tomorrow with Klaudia's Student Showcase, to which they were all invited. A van would come at eight a.m. sharp tomorrow morning to collect the wardrobe and take it to the college. Until then, Klaudia was locked away in her room, adding the final touches to her self-portrait.

'I'm going to sleep until noon every morning,'

said Clover dreamily, over breakfast, 'for the whole holiday.'

'I'm going to learn how to stilt-walk for the KFC,' said Tinkerbell. 'Only short ones made out of bean tins to start with,' she added, seeing Mum's face, 'till I know how not to fall off.'

'Well, I'm going to finish this dratted scene,' said Mum. (Apparently she was at the most difficult part of *Mermaid Girls 5: Snowflake Island*, where she needed to reveal the fiendish villain who controlled all the sea monsters. Villains were apparently much harder to conjure up than mermaids, and the disappearance of the Special Writing Mug was not helping.)

Pea said nothing. She didn't have plans. There wasn't anything she wanted to do; not now.

'You all right, Pea-hen?' said Mum gently. 'You've hardly eaten a thing.'

Pea looked at her cornflakes. She'd left them so long, they'd gone all bloaty and wet.

'Are you poorly?' asked Clover.

'Are you going to be sick?' asked Tinkerbell. 'In your breakfast?'

Pea shook her head. 'I'm not poorly, I'm fine,' she said, in a very small voice.

'Hmm,' said Mum. And she took Pea by the shoulders and steered her into the study.

'I need to brush my teeth – I'll be late for school,' protested Pea feebly, but Mum closed the door.

'If you're late, I'll write you a note,' she said, moving a pile of page proofs off a chair so they could both sit down. 'But I think you and me having a little talk's probably more important. Besides, no one ever does any work on the last day of school.'

Pea knew that wouldn't be true. Mr Ellis had promised them the hardest test of the whole term.

'Oh, Pea-nut, you've gone all pale!' Mum leaned in closer and took hold of her hands, pressing them tightly between her own warm ones. 'What is it, my lovely girl? You've not been yourself for ages.'

Pea looked down at her shoes. 'I'm not really sure who I am any more,' she said quietly. 'I tried being a writer and I wasn't good enough at that, so then I thought I should be a pet therapist, but I'm not cut out for the times when it goes wrong, if you see what I mean. So I tried being a footballer, and I *was* good at it, but I got bored. And I can't be an artist because I'll never be as good as Klaudia or Sam One. So now I'm just a nothing.'

Mum looked shocked. For a moment she said nothing at all; just kept holding Pea's hands very, very tightly. Then she reached into a drawer in her writing desk and pulled out a large bar of milk chocolate with whole hazelnuts in.

'Emergency chocolate,' she said, snapping off two squares for each of them. 'And yes, I know it's breakfast time, but my brilliant Pea thinking she's a nothing is *definitely* an emergency.'

Pea bit into her chocolate and felt a very tiny bit better.

'Now,' said Mum seriously. 'How on earth did

all this happen, darling? I knew you were trying out new things with your CV – but I thought that was all a sort of game. You're only eleven! Whatever made you think you had to decide what to do with the rest of your life right now?'

Pea munched on a hazelnut, thinking, then swallowed hard.

'After Klaudia came, we all thought we needed to make proper plans for the future, or we might end up with the wrong one. Like you did,' she added in a mumble.

Mum gasped. 'But sweetheart – oh, I didn't end up with the wrong future. How could you ever think that?'

Pea tugged on the long, loopy purple scarf draped around Mum's neck. 'Now you always wear dangly earrings and clothes like Klaudia's, and you'd much rather be drawing than writing . . .'

Mum snapped off another square of chocolate and popped it whole into her mouth, her cheeks going pink in two spots. When she'd finished munching, she took a deep breath and held Pea's hands again.

'Just because I wanted to study art when I was younger doesn't mean I didn't want to be a writer too. And a mum. Oh, more than anything I wanted to be a mum. And now look: I'm doing them all.' She waved her hand across her desk. There were handwritten notes on printed chapters; drawings of mermaid tails and pirate ships; and photographs, in frames, of Clover and Pea and Tinkerbell.

'No one has to be only one thing in their life, darling,' said Mum. 'I'm still an artist, even if I don't do it for my job. I'd still be a writer, even if all the *Mermaid Girls* books were just stories I'd written in a notebook to read to my girls. I'll always be a mum – even when I'm busy being a teacher, or a friend, or that annoying woman in the shop queue who's forgotten her PIN number. I can be all of them, all at the same time.'

Pea stared at her. Laid out like that, it seemed so obvious. Clem was an estate agent, *and* a dad, *and* a Birmingham City fan. Klaudia was an artist through and through – you could tell just by looking at her – but her wardrobe was meant to be a self-portrait, and it wasn't only paint pots and drawings.

'You don't have to choose what you're going to do with the rest of your life right now, my chick, because it'll be lots of different things,' said Mum. 'So stop fretting about all that. And as for *who* you are – well, you never have to choose that. You just get to *be* it. Do you see?'

Pea nodded, and Mum swept her up in a warm, jasminy hug; the special squeezy-tight sort.

She could go back to being Pea: Pea who didn't really like football, even if she was good at it; Pea who loved animals, even if she couldn't read their minds; Pea who liked to do art, even if she was rubbish. Perhaps even the Pea who liked books, and sometimes wrote stories. She could just *be*, without having to try to be *something*. Everything was going to be all right, after all.

Suddenly Mum sat back, a frown on her face. 'Hang on. Who told you you're not good enough to be a writer?'

Pea blushed, and explained about the *Spark!* website competition, and about awful Mr Ellis. Her voice went croaky when she got to the part about 6 out of 50, and 'Owls'.

There was a knock on the study door. Mum opened it, to find Clover with her coat on.

'Klaudia's locked in her room so I got Dr Paget to take Tink to school. Is Pea coming? Only I'll be late for the bus.'

'Oh, Pea's coming to school – and so am I,' said Mum, looking rather fierce. 'I think it's time me and your English teacher had a little chat.'

It felt very odd, sitting on the same old school bus she rode every day with Clover, only with Mum there too. It felt even odder walking through the Greyhope's gates with Mum sweeping ahead of them, flowing blonde hair and drapy scarves billowing. Pea spotted Bethany and Molly watching, curious, and gave them a small anxious wave.

'He'll be terribly stern and menacing,' breathed Clover approvingly as she disappeared off to her form room.

It was only five minutes before first bell, but Mum marched straight past the huddle of students outside Mr Ellis's room, and demanded he explain his wild passion for underlining and making people talk about 'Cheese'.

Pea waited outside, feeling very nervous. After a little while, she peered through the classroom door's window, trying to hear.

Mr Ellis's face – long dark hair, stubbly chin, cruel blue eyes and the flash of a gold earring – appeared at the door. Pea squeaked as he flung it open and beckoned her in with one ringed finger. Mum smiled reassuringly as Pea went to sit next to her, but she still felt nervous – especially when she saw a pile of her worksheets and grammar tests from the term piled on the desk.

'It seems,' said Mr Ellis grimly, 'that we have a small misunderstanding. Prude— I'm sorry, *Pea*: I happen to have just written your end-of-term report. Perhaps you'd like to read it yourself.'

He handed her a printed page.

PRUDENCE LLEWELLYN

ENGLISH – Mr E. Ellis

A very promising student. Prudence is shy, and Oral Presentations are not her strong suit, but I already see some improvement. Her written work is of a very high standard. She underachieves under test conditions and needs to improve her knowledge of grammar, but she should be very pleased with her performance this term.

Pea read it three times, just to be sure. 'Did you make him write this, just now?' she whispered to Mum.

'No!' said Mum, with a little smile. 'But perhaps the fact that you asked might tell Mr Ellis something. Hmm?'

She looked at Mr Ellis very pointedly, until he coughed. It was the first time Pea had ever seen him look the slightest bit flustered.

'Yes. Well,' he said, coughing again. 'I'm a great believer in challenging students . . . setting very high standards—'

'Making children think they're hopeless for no reason?' said Mum.

'No, no, of course I'd never . . .' Mr Ellis tried flicking his hair back and flashing his blue eyes, the way he did whenever the Year Nines were being rowdy in the playground, but Mum merely blinked. He turned to Pea instead, with a sigh. 'I never give full marks, Pea. It demotivates the students – makes them feel it's all too easy. In my, er, professional opinion. So, in my classroom, no one will ever get an A grade, or more than twenty-five out of fifty.'

'But I got six out of fifty in the first test you gave us,' said Pea.

Mr Ellis coughed, and explained that the first test of the year had been for him, to find out what the class knew, and what they'd clearly never been taught before. No one could possibly have done well.

'So I'm not awful at English?' said Pea, her heart swelling with hope.

Mr Ellis smiled weakly. 'You aren't much use at public speaking, though I think you know that. But no, you're not awful at English.'

Mum shot her a grin. Then she gave Mr Ellis a very severe look, shook his hand, and informed him that Pea would be unavailable for the rest of school today due to a family commitment.

'What family commitment?' asked Pea as Mum went to sign her out.

'Some Mum-and-Pea time,' said Mum. 'I need my best junior editor's help with this last chapter. You know my fearsome villain – the one I was having trouble with? Well, I think I've got him perfectly now. Let's see: long dark hair, blue eyes, silly gold earring . . . the Dread Pirate Ellis!'

It was the perfect way to spend a day. Mum let Pea read all of *Mermaid Girls 5: Snowflake Island* so far, curled up on a cushion with Wuffly's hairy nose tucked under her chin. (It was very good, even the scary parts with the skeletons in the cave.) They had lunch on their laps in front of the TV. Then Mum set to work on writing the Dread Pirate Ellis into her next chapter – who, she assured Pea, was about to be swallowed up by a huge sea monster with tentacles and pointy teeth. Pea went up to her little attic bedroom and lay on her bed re-reading the very first *Mermaid Girls* book.

Clover and Tinkerbell came home from school, full of end-of-term glee, but Pea stayed where she was, happily miles away on a beach filled with mermaids.

Dear Diary,

I've missed you! Now I know about Mr Ellis I feel a bit silly for giving up on writing (even though Mum says that's mainly his fault, and he is a grown-up so he should feel sillier).

Tomorrow is the Easter holidays. I'm going to start a new story about pirates in space, or maybe angels. Who might be in space, or not. It's been so long since I've written a story I've got nearly too many ideas. Maybe I can give one or two to Sam One for him to draw instead.

I'm going to re-read every single book on my book shelf (starting with Mum's), and then I'm going to go to Kilburn Library to read all of theirs too.

Also I am going to write in you, dear Diary, every day. It is a promise.

Love from Pea xx

As Pea put down her pen, she heard a strange yet familiar rumbling.

She tried picking up her book again, but there it was: a throbbing, pulsing hum coming from downstairs. Klaudia's old shouty German rock music, that's what it was; once Pea opened her bedroom door she could even hear the guitars.

She headed for the kitchen. The music was so loud, the glasses in the kitchen cupboards were rattling together. Tinkerbell was sitting on the kitchen table with her fingers in her ears, while Mum and Clover hammered on Klaudia's door.

'I don't think she can hear you!' shouted Pea.

'*What?*' shouted Mum.

'I said—' Pea began again, even louder.

The music stopped abruptly.

The door was flung open – to reveal Klaudia, her eyes huge like boiled eggs, still wearing the same clothes she'd had on yesterday.

'Can't stop now,' she said, in a vaguely sinister

voice, staring straight past them. 'Not ready. Not finished. Need more time.'

She began to push the door shut, but Mum stuck out a foot and blocked it.

'Klaudia, darling,' she said, patting her on the arm very gently, as if she were a dog that might bite. 'I think you've been working a bit too hard, hmm?'

Klaudia scratched her own face as if she were scratching someone else's. Flakes of paint flew up. There was the underneath half of a Jammy Dodger stuck to her arm.

'Artists,' sighed Clover.

They'd all seen Mum in a similar state at the end of a book, or while waiting for the Dreaditor to send notes. She even had a special outfit for it, nicknamed the Sad Dress: a shapeless floor-length thing with lots of pockets, most of which contained empty chocolate wrappers (and once, to universal horror, a tiny snail).

Klaudia noticed the Jammy Dodger, then

peeled it off and lifted it towards her mouth.

'Whoa,' said Mum, carefully taking it out of her hand. 'Let's not. Why don't you go and have a shower, and then I'll take you out for some fresh air, all right?'

She grabbed Klaudia's crutches, and tugged and prodded her back inside towards her little bathroom, wrinkling her nose all the way. Clover pulled back the curtains and opened a window to let some air into the fuggy room. The wardrobe was still in the middle of the floor, now even more stuffed with cushions and oddments than when Pea had filmed it. Tinkerbell was staring at it with a rather unimpressed expression – so Pea pushed the hangers apart to reveal the painted back with the starry sky and the picture of their street.

'Oooh,' breathed Tinkerbell. 'OK. It's still weird, but I like it now.'

'Isn't that Mum's Special Writing Mug?' said Clover.

There it was, dangling from one of the coat-hangers. They debated whether to rescue it, but Pea thought Mum wouldn't mind sacrificing it in the name of art.

Twenty minutes later, a clean, dressed but still dazed Klaudia emerged.

'Right, then,' said Mum. 'You need a change of scenery, a bit of company, and not to be thinking about tomorrow at all. I've already called your friend Aimee; she's going to meet us in the pub with a few friends.'

Klaudia was too robotic to even protest.

'Clover's in charge,' Mum called, coaxing Klaudia awkwardly down the crazy paving. 'Pizza money on the side. Phone me if there's an emergency. And Tink, take that monster dog for a walk, please!'

Tinkerbell took Wuffly for a two-minute stroll around the garden, then flopped in front of the TV. They ordered ham and pineapple pizza and lots of cheesy garlic bread, and ate it watching *Toy Story 3*.

A few hours later, Mum phoned to check the house was not on fire, from somewhere very noisy. 'We might be a bit late back!' she yelled into the phone, then broke off to talk to someone giggly in the background. 'Don't wait up! Ask Dr Paget if you need anything!'

Pea left Clover and Tinkerbell arguing over whether *Coronation Street* was better than watching *Toy Story 3* again, and went upstairs. It wasn't completely dark yet, but she put on her pyjamas and curled up on her bed with the rest of her book. She forgot all about Mum being out at the pub. She forgot about reminding Tinkerbell to brush her teeth and go to bed. She drifted off into her own mermaidy world. And then she drifted off to sleep. Pea's dream was full of pirate ships and dank, spooky caves. She was swimming through the water, flipping her fishy mermaid tail, into a firelit cavern filled with treasure and skeletons of the long-dead . . . Something was chasing her, a shape in the water – some kind of sea monster!

She swam faster, faster, but the shape was drawing closer and closer, clutching at her tail with its tentacles, gnashing its teeth, and making a long, howling wail that sent a horrible chill through her whole body.

Pea's eyes snapped open just in time. She wiggled her toes to make sure they were still there and she hadn't really turned mermaid. Then she shivered and closed her eyes, wrapping the duvet tighter around her shoulders.

But it came again, louder this time: a moaning, groaning, terrible sound. Not in a dream. Right here, in the house, downstairs.

Pea felt frozen all over.

What could it be?

She checked the clock. It was late – almost eleven – but she hadn't heard Mum come back. They were alone in the house, alone with some terrible *thing* . . . 'Clover? Tink?' she called, in a wobbly voice.

No answer. Only another howl from downstairs,

this time followed by a series of yelps and whimpers. Petrified, Pea tiptoed down the attic steps and along the corridor. She could hear Clover snoring, but Tinkerbell was not in her bed. She crept all the way downstairs. There was no one in the front room, or the study. The howling was coming from the back of the house, beyond the kitchen, from inside Klaudia's firmly shut bedroom door.

'Tink?' whispered Pea, tapping at the door. 'Tink, are you there? Are you . . . are you all right?'

'Yes!' shouted Tinkerbell from inside. There was a pause. 'Don't come in!'

Another terrible moaning sound emerged from behind the door.

With a shaky hand, Pea turned the handle. As she pushed it open, she scrunched up her eyes until they were almost closed, in case a terrible sea monster was about to unleash its tentacles and gobble her up.

What she saw was very nearly as terrifying.

Tinkerbell was kneeling on the floor, trembling, in front of Klaudia's wardrobe – or what was left of it. The sari fabric and red velvet cushions had been torn to shreds, leaving fluff and feathers scattered all over the carpet. The letters and clothes dangling from the hangers were ripped to bits. But there was no time to worry about that. Inside the wardrobe, nestled in the middle of all the fluff and wool, lying on her side with her fat belly all lumpy and her legs sticking out, was Wuffly, her eyes every bit as shiny and terrified as they had been when she was lying on the road outside after the accident.

Pea dropped to her knees to give Wuffly's head a comforting stroke – but Wuffly uncharacteristically snapped at her fingers until Pea snatched them back.

She gave another long low growling howl. Then a tiny black puppy seemed to grow out from under Wuffly's bottom, to land *flop* on the remains of the red velvet cushion.

Pea heard Tinkerbell gasp.

'Tink,' she whispered.

Tinkerbell reached out and grabbed her hand, and Pea could feel her quivering all over.

The tiny black thing wriggled and squirmed. Its eyes were closed and it looked very small, and baggy, and slightly pig-like. Wuffly shuffled and craned her neck round, then began to lick at it till it made a snuffly coughing noise.

'Don't be cross,' Tinkerbell said in a very quavery voice. 'I was going to tell everyone, honestly I was. I thought there wouldn't be any puppies for another few weeks – that's what your book from the school library says.' *Know Your Dog* was propped open beside her.

'But – Tink? How did this . . . ? When did . . . ?'

Tinkerbell looked tearful. 'It was an accident! Once when we took Wuffly to the park in the wheelie case, we let her out for a run and she got in a fight with another dog. I didn't realize until Dr Paget explained about those two rabbits, and how they weren't really fighting. But I thought we

281

could sell the puppies for the KFC and make lots of money. Mostly I thought someone would realize before any of this happened, only everyone just said Wuffly had got fat and didn't realize at all, and then tonight she got all poorly, and I knocked on the wall for someone to come but they didn't hear, and then Wuffly got upset and I didn't want to leave her, and . . .'

Wuffly whined sharply, and suddenly there was another tiny black puppy, *flop*, on top of the other one.

'How many will there be?' asked Pea.

In the book of *The Hundred and One Dalmatians*, Missis had given birth to fifteen puppies. Pea wasn't sure that was actually possible in real life, but it would be comforting to know what to expect.

Tinkerbell shook her head. 'Don't know. It might be only two. But it could be ten.'

Pea swallowed hard. Ten was almost as many as fifteen.

'What's all the noise about? I'm trying to— Oh!'

Clover had appeared in the doorway, her face still crumply from bed. She looked very wide awake now, though.

'Don't tell Mum!' squeaked Tinkerbell.

'Mum's not here,' said Pea, suddenly feeling frightened as Wuffly made another low growling sound, and her legs jerked.

Clover looked at Pea, her face paling. Pea looked helplessly back at her, feeling utterly lost. It was just like immediately after the car accident: as if things were happening in a dream, and she couldn't step out of it. Only there was no Mum around to tell her what to do; no one but themselves. Pea tried telling herself to be brave, like she had at the accident – but somehow it didn't make any difference. There was a terrible, scary pause.

Then Clover stuck out her chin and tied her hair up off her face. 'Right. We'll have to sort this out ourselves till Mum gets back, then,' she said briskly, in a very Mum-like tone of voice. 'Pea, go and phone Mum, then find the number of the vee-ee-tee. Tinkerbell, fetch blankets. Do puppies need blankets?'

Tinkerbell flipped through *Know Your Dog*. 'I think they need a box that's warm and cosy. You're supposed to get one ready; that's why Wuffly went in the wardrobe – to make her own, because I hadn't done it yet . . .' Then she darted to her feet. 'I know what to use.'

She hurried upstairs.

Pea called Mum, but there was no reply, so she left a message ('*No one's dead or on fire, but there's a sort of a thing happening which isn't very good, so please come home right away. Please, it's very urgent. This is Pea, by the way!*'), and texted as well, just in case Mum was still somewhere very noisy.

By the time she came back, another small black puppy had popped out. Wuffly was hunched over them, licking the sticky stuff off their fur.

'It's all right, she's meant to do that,' said

Clover, rapidly reading *Know Your Dog*. 'And it says you don't need a vee-ee-tee unless the mother is in distress or one of the puppies gets stuck. OK, sit down, Pea, you've gone a funny colour. Well done, Wuffly, good girl. Ooh, Tink, that's brilliant! Where did that come from?'

Tinkerbell had reappeared clutching a heavy cardboard box. She turned it upside-down, and hundreds of magazines spilled out across the carpet. One of them fell open, to reveal Clover's terrible Angelhair shampoo advert. 'Sorry,' she said.

Clover took a deep breath, then shook herself. 'Best use for them,' she said firmly, and began to tear the pages into strips to fill up the cardboard box.

Then Wuffly gave another long growly moan and, very slowly, puppy number four arrived. This one was smaller than all the others, and it took a lot of licking from Wuffly (and a bit of help from Clover, rubbing its tummy with a clean cloth like it said in the book) to get it to wriggle like the others, but soon it was snuffling away.

Wuffly went on groaning and whining for quite some while, but no more puppies appeared.

By the time Mum came dashing through the front door, Wuffly and all four puppies were lying comfortably in the cardboard box, lined with the beloved blue blanket and torn-up bits of Clover's advert.

'What? What is it? What's happened? What—?' shouted Mum, barrelling down the corridor in a panic. She skidded into the kitchen, then stood in the doorway to Klaudia's room, blinking at the scene as if her eyes couldn't quite take in what they were seeing.

'We're all right, Mum,' said Clover soothingly. 'I did the calm-in-a-crisis thing, like Pea did before.'

'Wuffly had puppies,' explained Pea.

'I'm really, really sorry,' said Tinkerbell, in a whisper.

Mum sank to her knees. Her face went from relief, to confusion, to the kind of stern anger that only Tinkerbell could produce. Then one of the puppies made a snuffly noise, its little pink tongue poking out of its mouth, and Mum couldn't help but smile fondly at it.

'Oh, my horrors, I'm never going out of the house again,' she whispered, sweeping them all into a hug.

Behind her, there was a thump and a clatter as Klaudia sat down hard on a chair and dropped her crutches.

'My self-portrait,' she whispered, her mouth falling open. 'My wardrobe. It's . . . gone.'

CHAPTER
13

A WORK OF ART

No one got much sleep.

Mum tried sending them all upstairs with hot cocoa, but Tinkerbell wouldn't leave the puppies, and Clover didn't want to leave Tinkerbell to deal with them all alone. Klaudia had sunk back into her robot state, and couldn't be moved from her kitchen chair. In the end, Pea brought all the duvets downstairs, and the sisters slept in Klaudia's bedroom, listening to the odd snuffly breaths of Wuffly's babies.

Pea woke up cold and uncomfortable, with Clover's toes poking her in the back. She tried going back to sleep, but it was light outside, and she could hear Mum's voice on the phone in the corridor.

After quickly checking the cardboard box – Wuffly was fast asleep, quite worn out – Pea crept away into the hallway.

'Yes, I do see, yes,' said Mum solemnly into the phone. 'Even if it wasn't her fault? Hmm. And there's nothing at all you can do to change that?'

She lifted a finger to her lips to shush Pea, and jerked her head towards the front room. Inside, Pea could see an exhausted-looking Klaudia lying sprawled on her back on the sofa, snoring softly.

'I see. Yes . . . Before nine a.m., yes . . . OK, thank you.' Mum hung up the phone, her face looking bleak. 'I've just been talking to one of Klaudia's professors. If Klaudia doesn't produce a piece for the showcase, she'll fail her course.'

'What?' Pea clapped her hand over her mouth as Klaudia stirred, and Mum tugged her along the corridor to the quiet of the kitchen. 'But that's not fair! It wasn't her fault!' Pea hissed.

'I know, darling. There must be something we can do. Maybe we can try to put it back together?'

They tiptoed round the sleeping people (and dogs) to look at the wardrobe. There was a funny smell coming from the raggedy cushions, and Wuffly's paws had scratched great chunks out of the paintwork. When Mum touched one of the doors, the golden picture frame attached to it fell off in her hand.

'That's that, then,' she said miserably. 'She can't showcase this.'

Looking at the painting on the back panel, Pea felt her heart sink. It wasn't just the thought that Klaudia might fail her exam. It was the way she'd talked about her work, all her inspiration, when Pea had been filming her, her eyes bright and sparky with excitement . . .

'Oh!' said Pea, clapping her hand to her mouth again. 'I – I think I might know how Klaudia can take her wardrobe to the showcase, after all!'

She went to find Klaudia's coat and took out her phone.

Three more phone calls later, it was all arranged.

Mum woke Klaudia, and promised her they had a nice surprise waiting for her at the college. Pea woke Clover and Tinkerbell and explained the plan. Tinkerbell hurried next door, and returned with Sams One and Two and Dr Paget, who promised to stay on puppy-watching duty.

By half past eight they were all yawning on the bus.

'I'm really, really, really properly sorry about your wardrobe,' said Tinkerbell.

'Mmm,' said Klaudia vaguely, looking out of the window. She was wearing her usual array of bright mismatched clothes, but she looked somehow blurry and indistinct today. It was as if losing the self-portrait had taken a part of her Klaudia-ness away with it.

'You'd better be sorry,' said Mum, giving Tinkerbell a stare. 'You and I are going to have a very long discussion when we get home, Stinks. No chocolate for you for at least a year. And don't think for an instant we're going to keep those puppies – though how we're going to find them all homes . . . Oh, how did I not notice that Wuffly was pregnant?'

They got off at their usual stop. The college looked quite different today, though: it was buzzing with people, and they had to get Klaudia to show a special ID card to let them in a back entrance.

Inside, a short round woman with frizzles of grey in her black hair started frantically waving at Pea.

'Are you Aditi? We spoke on the phone,' said Mum as Klaudia hobbled over on one crutch.

'Yes!' she said, shaking Mum's hand warmly. 'It all came through perfectly, yes, and one of the other students got it all set up. And of course I recognize *you*,' she added confusingly, shaking Pea's hand too. 'Such a lovely piece, you know. Going to be the star of the show, I think!'

Pea looked uncertainly at Mum, who was looking just as confused – but Aditi led them down the long white room, past the zigzag coat (which was now being worn by its artist, who had painted his face blue for the occasion), past the horse made of wire (now covered in flower petals, as if it had bloomed overnight). Each student had a small area to themselves, with their name on a card on the floor. Klaudia's space was all the way down the far end, and they almost couldn't see her name on the card for the crowd of people gathered there – drawn by the sound of Klaudia's voice, excitedly talking about 'the found art of the doll's house', echoing out of a speaker somewhere.

'I set the projector up on a loop, Klaudia, dear – I assume that's what you wanted? So clever, such a distinctive signature.' Aditi patted Klaudia's arm, apparently not noticing her glazed expression, and pushed them in front of the gathered crowd.

The floor space where Klaudia's wardrobe was to go was, of course, empty. But on the bare white wall behind it was projected the video Pea had taken, two metres tall.

It was not, however, a video of the almost-finished wardrobe. Klaudia's happy voice was the soundtrack – but the picture was of Pea's own face, her mouth a little open as she listened, a tiny frown between her eyes as she concentrated on holding the phone's camera up.

'Oh, Pea-pod,' whispered Mum in her ear. 'You must've switched the phone to use the camera at the front, not the back. You filmed yourself instead of the wardrobe.'

'We haven't rescued the self-portrait at all,' whispered Clover, looking at Pea in despair.

Pea could only stare in horror as her huge freckly face stared back at the crowd from the wall. Then there was a flicker, and the film restarted from the beginning. She could hear her own voice asking if Klaudia was ready; saw herself suck on her bottom lip as she steadied the camera and nodded for Klaudia to begin. Then the image wobbled as Pea moved around, her face still the only thing on the screen as Klaudia described velvet and feathers; origami frogs and birthday necklaces. None of them were on the screen, but as Klaudia talked, Pea's face made all sorts of little responses – an eye-brow-raise here, a tiny quirk of a smile there. When Klaudia pulled back the hangers to reveal the painted panel, Pea's eyes went wide and shiny, her awe as obvious as if it had been written down.

'Look,' whispered Tinkerbell, tugging on Pea's sleeve.

Pea looked. The crowd were all nodding slowly, beginning to smile.

It was as if it didn't matter that the wardrobe itself wasn't there. Pea's reaction to it was appar-ently every bit as interesting to look at. When Klaudia's voice started to explain about perspec-tive and technique, Pea's eyes flicked sideways, her mouth twisting slightly in disappointment, and a ripple of laughter passed through the crowd. Pea blushed, but Mum was smiling too – as if she and all the others were thinking, like Pea had, that it was a shame that it wasn't simply a beautiful picture.

Then the giant Pea-face on the wall blinked, and tilted its head sideways, and smiled again as Klaudia's passionate voice grew quicker and more excitable, as if it were coming to some new bigger understanding. When the real Pea looked at Mum, the exact same expression was passing across her face too.

'Oh, that Aditi was right,' she murmured. 'It *is* clever.'

'It's like art that shows you *your*self, instead of *it*self,' said Pea slowly. 'Is that right?'

'Art that goes outwards,' breathed Clover, remembering what Klaudia had told them at the very first art class.

'Like a mirror you've never seen before,' said

Klaudia faintly. Then, to Pea's astonishment, she broke into a peal of giddy laughter. 'Ha! *Ha!* Genius! It's, like, so much better this way! The wardrobe, you know, it was all about *me* – too insular, too personal. But this – it's . . . it's . . .'

'Nuts?' suggested Tinkerbell.

'Yeah!' said Klaudia. 'Don't you love it!'

The video froze for a moment on Pea's face, flickered, then turned to black before beginning the loop again. This time, the assembled crowd broke out into applause.

'Look, there she is!' said someone.

Suddenly Pea found herself swamped. Everyone there wanted to ask her a question about the installation. But Mum firmly pushed Klaudia in front of Pea, telling them *she* was the artist – and Klaudia began to talk avidly about her inspiration, and her artistic approach, and how the piece had come about. She even told the waiting crowd about Wuffly and the puppies, and how the art they'd just heard talked about no longer even existed – which

297

somehow, the way she described it, made it sound even more special and exciting.

'Come on,' whispered Pea. 'We should go. This is Klaudia's big moment.'

Mum smiled, and nodded. They crept away, leaving Klaudia quite surrounded by people, all very keen to shake her hand and ask about her future plans.

The two bus trips home were silent. Everyone was exhausted but happy. They stopped off at the café round the corner on the way back, and returned with an enormous mountain of hot bacon baps for the puppy-sitters, and lots of coffee for Mum. They ate them sitting around the kitchen table, while Clover told everyone the story of the birth of the puppies, and the wardrobe, and Pea's unexpectedly brilliant film. Sam One and Sam Two sat on the floor with Wuffly, pausing between bites of bacon bap to chase another escaping puppy as it tumbled out of the cardboard nest.

'Mum Gen's called round lots of people,' said

Sam One, 'and we think we've found homes for three of the puppies – though they'll have to stay here for quite a while first so they can be with their mum.'

'And you might not need to find a home for the last one,' said Sam Two, holding the smallest puppy up to her cheek, its eyes looming big in its face.

'Not so fast!' said Dr Paget, glaring at Sam Two; then, turning apologetically to Mum, 'Kara can't bear dogs, you see, she's always hated them. I don't think . . .'

'She couldn't not love this one!'

Sam Two deposited the puppy on Dr Paget's lap. The puppy climbed up her chest, sniffling at her long dangly necklace. Then it nuzzled her under the chin. Dr Paget gave its head a tentative stroke with one fingertip.

'I suppose we have recommended aversion therapy for our patients before now . . .' she said doubtfully.

'Have you ever looked after a puppy before,

Sam?' asked Mum. 'Because it's quite a lot of work. Although I suppose if you needed some help . . . Hmm, who do we know who's good with a dog . . . ?'

Mum and Dr Paget exchanged looks as Sam Two narrowed her eyes at Tinkerbell.

'I suppose you could come over to hang out every now and then,' said Sam Two, shuffling her shoulders. 'If you wanted to help with the puppy.'

Tinkerbell beamed.

'How perfect: one of Wuffly's babies will be right next door,' said Clover, scruffling Wuffly's ears fondly.

'Yay! What are we going to call it?' said Sam Two to Sam One.

Sam One thought hard. 'How about . . . Surprise?'

'Stop naming it!' said Dr Paget. 'We might not be keeping it!'

'Yeah, we so are,' said Sam Two confidently.

Surprise the puppy turned round in Dr Paget's lap, nestled its head into the palm of her hand, and promptly fell asleep. Its little nose twitched. Its tail wagged once, sharply, at whatever had appeared in a dream.

Dr Paget gazed down, then sighed. 'Oh, I give up.'

Sam One and Sam Two beamed.

'So, how does it feel to be a walking work of art, Pea?' asked Dr Paget, grinning as she absently stroked the puppy's tail.

'Um,' said Pea. 'Not very different from being ordinary, really.'

Mum drained her coffee cup and thumped it down on the table. 'Oof, it's a good thing I never did bother with being an art student,' she yawned. 'They do stay up awfully late.'

'But you'll carry on with Klaudia's drawing classes next term, though, won't you?' said Pea. 'Because you can be more than one thing. I mean, you can be an art student *and* a mermaidy writer, right?'

Mum rubbed her eyes, then nodded and stroked

Pea's frizzly ponytail. 'Someone very clever must have told you that, I think. Yes, maybe I will.'

'Will there be naked ladies next time?' asked Sam One. 'Because personally I prefer drawing spaceships and ants and that sort of thing.'

Clover blinked. 'I'm *so* glad I gave up modelling.'

Mum laughed, and gave Clover a kiss on the cheek. 'Me too, my angel.'

'I'm going to keep being a funraisin, though,' said Tinkerbell. 'The KFC's all skint again.'

'I'll help,' said Clover brightly. 'I could ask Drama Club to do a special charity performance. A musical! We could sell tickets, and make crispy cakes to sell at the interval – or something else that's not so boring. I'll be the star. And Pea could write the story – I mean, if you wanted to, Pea.' She hesitated. 'What do you think?'

Pea looked at her tatty old CV, still pinned to the fridge, and smiled. 'I think I'd like to, lots,' she said.

PEA

Age: 11

Current occupation: schoolgirl

Likes: books

Special skills: writing, reading,
    making sandwiches

Future career: ~~writer (like Mum)~~ ?

~~pet therapist~~ ?

~~footballer~~ ?

~~artist~~ ?

puppy deliverer

work of art

friend

sister

daughter

author of 'KFC: the Musical'

?

?

?

Join Pea on her BIG MOVE TO LONDON
and her quest to find a new best friend.
(Which is harder than it sounds . . .)

Warning! This book is not about mermaids.

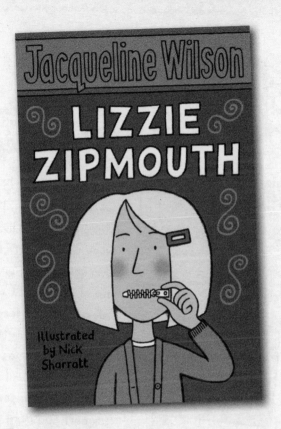

Lizzie refuses to speak. She doesn't want to talk to Rory or Jake, her new stepbrothers. Or to Sam, their dad. Or even to her mum. She's completely fed up with having to join a new family, and nothing can convince her to speak to them. Not football, not pizza, not a new bedroom. That is, until she meets a member of the new family who is even more stubborn than she is – and has had a lot more practice!

The Lady Grace Mysteries

My name is Lady Grace Cavendish, and I'm Her Majesty Queen Elizabeth's favourite Maid of Honour. Everyone thinks growing up at the Royal Court is all parties and feasts and jewels – but mysterious, dangerous things always seem to happen! And because I am small and smart and very good at sneaking around, the Queen has made me her own special secret investigator.

Last night was the Valentine's Ball, and I was supposed to pick a suitor there (boring!). But later on, one of them was found dead – with a dagger in his back! And it's up to me to find the killer . . .

The Lady Grace Mysteries

When Grace's fellow Maid of Honour, Lady Sarah, disappears after a trip to meet the Queen's fleet in the docks, Grace knows she has to find out what's going on. She believes Sarah has run away to be married to the handsome Captain Drake – but is she right? With the help of her acrobat friend Masou, Grace leaves the court in disguise in an attempt to track down Lady Sarah and try to save her honour. But this time Grace may be taking on more than she can cope with, as she faces life at sea, and the dangers of pirates! Will Grace and Masou ever return from their ill-fated voyage?

**Alice-Miranda Highton-Smith-Kennington-Jones
is waving goodbye to her parents and starting her
first day at boarding school.**

But something is wrong at Winchesterfield-Downsfordvale
Academy for Proper Young Ladies. The headmistress, Miss
Grimm, hasn't been seen for ten years. A mysterious stranger
is camping in the greenhouse. And Alice-Miranda has to
complete a series of impossible, dangerous challenges.

**Can Alice-Miranda pass each test and uncover the school's
secrets? Well, of course. This is Alice-Miranda, after all.**

**Alice-Miranda has survived her first
term at boarding school.**

And now her friend Jacinta Headlington-Bear,
the school's second best tantrum thrower, is joining
Alice-Miranda at Highton Hall for the half-term
holiday. But who is the cranky boy who throws stones
at them? And why is a handsome movie star sneaking
around the garden late at night?

**Alice-Miranda might have a more exciting
holiday than she expected . . .**